KEIF'S

Pack

BRENNA LYONS

FIREBORN
PUBLISHING

Fireborn Publishing Copyright Statement

PUBLISHER

FIREBORN
PUBLISHING

**PO Box 5216
Haverhill, MA 01835**

Section One

A Buck's Apology

Prologue

This story was one I wrote as a free read, to introduce the Keif's Pack world. I hope you enjoy. While it is only obliquely related to the other stories in the world, it does give insights into wolf hierarchy that readers may find useful.

Happy reading!
Brenna

"No buck relinquishes his solitude quietly or willingly."

How many times had I heard those words and never really understood what they signified? I'd foolishly believed bucks moaned and groaned about the loss of their freedom but—like she-wolves—went to mating with a sense of relief. That they reveled in finding their fated mates.

How wrong I'd been. Kole had come to me angry. Royally—if you'll pardon the pun—pissed off at losing his bachelor lifestyle. Sex had been rough and fast, though repeated. There'd been no sweetness, no fireworks, and certainly no discussion.

Like all alpha bucks that encounter their mates high cycle, Kole had taken what he wanted. Unlike all bucks I personally knew, he'd left my personal den within moments of regaining his senses—right about the time I'd laid my return mating mark on the meat of his bicep—and hadn't taken me to his own.

A quarter moon later, I hadn't seen my "mate" again. *The jerk!* Here I was, in a predictable state for a female who had mated during high cycle, and no mate that cared to claim me. To top it, Kole had destroyed one of my favorite outfits in his haste to have what he wanted.

In some sick way, I had to admire Kole's fortitude. It was *supposedly* impossible for him to walk away from his mate, but he'd managed it.

I wondered what he would do when it came time to induct my pups into the den, and his sire realized who'd sired the young ones. When the old buck realized that I carried Kole's mating mark but wasn't properly claimed by his precious heir. It wasn't going to be a pretty scene.

Kole's sire might banish him for being so thoughtless and uncaring of his mate's feelings. It was unlikely, but it was possible. Kole had two younger siblings capable of becoming the new alpha.

Worse, the old buck might try to force Kole to take on his responsibilities. They could both forget it! If Kole didn't come to me and make a really big show of subservience, there was no way I was going to accept him back. He'd turned his back on me and our pups together. I could do the same to him. In fact, his callous dismissal of us made that decision a very easy one to come to. There was certainly no love lost between us.

And if the old alpha turns me out? That caused my heart to stutter, and I swallowed a lump in my throat.

There are other packs. There are other dens within the pack. Kole's sire wasn't Tragen of the entire pack, and the Tragen might welcome a new female to his den. For that matter, most dens would do the same. It was much harder for a rogue buck to find a new home than a rogue female, pups in tow or not. I wouldn't even have to change packs to find a new home, most likely.

The male body sliding into position at my shoulder caused me to jump, and I turned with every intention of taking a hunk of buck hide out, whether that buck was Kole or not.

Joshua caught my clawed hand with a smirk. "And good evening to you, Jellica."

I snatched my hand away and growled at him. "It's good when bucks mind their manners and don't touch what isn't theirs." Still, out of common courtesy, I allowed my claws to shift back into human fingernails.

"Are you someone's to touch?"

The flaring of his nostrils prompted another growl from me. He was taking in my scent, confirming what had likely drawn him to me in the first place—the novelty of what appeared to be an unmated female bearing pups.

Damn him, and damn all bucks! Most of all, damn his overactive sense of smell. Most wolves would miss my gravid state for at least another week or two.

3

"I speak for myself, and I say I am not yours to touch." I started to round him, intent on a rest in my personal den.

He captured my wrist again, drawing me to a stop. "Good. No buck speaks for you. Then let me make myself clear."

I sighed then ground my teeth in frustration. "If you must." It was unlikely to change anything, but he could say whatever he felt the want to.

"You know my mate is dead."

I hadn't, and the pronouncement made my heart skip a beat and my cheeks heat. It must have happened in the years he'd been gone from the den—mated and left alone before they could even produce young. It was heartbreaking.

Joshua continued, most likely content I would hear him out now. He wasn't incorrect about it.

"My mate is dead, and you carry young. Young I would claim as my own...and you with them, were you willing to entertain such an idea."

My head spun at the pronouncement. Though our kind were known to raise the abandoned or orphaned young of others, it was an unprecedented move to offer to raise the young of an unknown quantity.

Could I entertain such an offer?

Why not? My mind raged. *Kole has shown no interest in this mating. If I was settled with another male, his sire wouldn't try to force us together, and I wouldn't be forced into the situation of leaving my close family.* It was an appealing prospect, and

4

Joshua was a more than appealing male specimen.

He had light fur and eyes, which set him apart from Kole and was strangely winsome in itself. Though he lacked the bulk of an alpha, Joshua was sturdy and lean, most probably quick, agile...an adequate hunter.

"I've shocked you," he stated lamely.

I nodded. "Yes. I think you have." *Just as useless a comment.* What was wrong with me? I should have simply agreed and been done with it. It certainly wasn't that I was waiting for Kole to make right what he'd destroyed. I had no kind feelings left for him. I opened my mouth to agree.

"I have already offered and I stand by that, but I must ask. Is there a buck that will try to speak for you? Will I be forced to fight for you?" Joshua hurried on. "I will willingly do so, and I will not lose this battle. But I must know... Have you ties to any wolf?"

"No ties I wish to be a part of," I answered honestly.

His grip on my wrist loosened, and he rubbed at my pulse point, raising more than a slight interest in me.

"You need time to consider my offer," Joshua guessed.

"Yes." Why I couldn't simply spit out the words was beyond me, and that was enough to convince me to take time to consider it.

Joshua tipped his head and started to withdraw. "As you wish, Jellica."

I gripped his hand as he pulled it away. "Making a decision would be easier if I knew you better. You have been gone most of my adolescence and adulthood." In fact, he was a full decade older than I was, but bucks were often much older than their mates.

His lips curved in a slight smile, and he offered his arm. "Of course. Would you like to walk in the moonlight for a bit?"

I wound my arm through his. "I would like that very much." It was a simple walk, but it was the start of something that might become much more.

****

Stepping back into the den from the lush forest cast something of a pall over my mood. The rational part of my mind argued I knew Joshua well enough to make a decision. A rebellious corner insisted this was nothing to rush into. I'd let the heat of the moment take over with Kole, and that hadn't ended well at all.

But how long would Joshua give me to make a decision? And was it cruel to give him hope of something I might ultimately deny him?

I opened my mouth to ask him for a bit more time. I couldn't decide if I really wanted the time or if I just wanted to see his reaction to the request.

The words never made it past my lips. Instead, my sire's voice brought me up short. "Ah. There you are. The alpha has called a meeting."

My throat went dry at the pronouncement. Had someone whelped a new litter of pups in an outlying den? Was there some tension with another den or pack? Had word come from the Tragen?

My only hope was that it had nothing to do with Kole and myself. *Not before I've formed a den with Joshua.*

As if the thought of the man's name spurred him, Joshua spoke. "When is this meeting?"

"Within the quarter hour. I suggest you both hurry." My sire glanced at our hooked arms and let a hint of a smile curve his lips.

Wonderful, I fumed. As soon as he told my dam about this, she would start giving me advice on bucks. *A little too late for that.*

Joshua tipped his head and led me past my sire and toward the gathering area.

A glance back confirmed that my sire had headed off in the direction of the personal den he shared with my dam. Any buck worth his while escorted his mate to such a function.

As Joshua is escorting me. Kole isn't looking for me. He isn't here to act as a proper mate. I should just accept Joshua. That resolved, I decided to do so directly after the meeting.

****

7

The gathering area was crowded when we arrived, half a hundred or more wolves in human form packed—excuse yet another pun—into the cavern. Joshua chose a spot for us near the back. I was relieved that he'd done so. The last thing I wanted was to draw the alpha's attention to me before I was settled with Joshua.

A murmur of voices surrounded us. Everywhere, people were passing news and speculating on what the alpha had to tell us. No one mentioned a new litter, but it was possible the affected den members were near the front of the crowd, and word hadn't yet filtered back to us.

The alpha walked out on the ledge overlooking the crowd, Kole at his side. Forcing my lip not to curl in disgust was difficult. *How dare he stand there, acting the part of dutiful heir, when he'd treated me so shamefully?*

It took a moment for the rest to come into focus. The old alpha bowed his head to Kole and backed away, a clear indication that they'd battled for leadership and Kole had come away the victor.

Kole started to speak, but I couldn't hear any of it over the pounding of my heart and the sickening rush of blood in my ears. It would be the same old assurances that he would lead the den honorably.

As if Kole has any honor!

Kole looked up, seemingly seeking something out in the crowd. His head slowed, reversed, and held...his gaze locked in my general direction. He

8

stopped speaking and his jaw tightened as if in rebuke.

Confused, I looked down at myself. My arm was still wound through Joshua's. It was a bold statement. It showed intent of something more.

And then it hit me. Kole didn't want me, but I wouldn't be able to make an agreement with Joshua either. The pups were Kole's heirs, and if I balked at whatever he decreed about them, I would be cast out. Though he couldn't take my young from me, he could banish all of us from his den.

I'll leave now. It was the safest course of action. That thought firmly in mind, I released Joshua's arm, turned, and bolted.

"Jellica!"

Joshua's shout followed me into the tunnels. I ignored it, my head spinning with plans. I would have to run alone. It would be much easier to get a den to take me in if I didn't come with a buck. Other bucks would willingly offer what Joshua had, once word spread that I carried an alpha's young. I could have my pick of attentive male bodies.

But I had to leave quickly, before Kole could seek me out. If he interfered, it would take longer for me to escape him. I would gather a few precious belongings and flee into the night air. It didn't matter where I went, as long as it wasn't under Kole's rule.

Tragen! If anyone could force Kole into retreat, it would be the local pack leader. He was alpha over all the den alphas.

It would mean living in a city dwelling, but I could accept that, if it meant my freedom.

My hands shaking wildly, I started snatching up clothing and shoving it into a large sack. Kole could have the den and everything left in it, but he would never own me or my pups.

"Jellica?" Joshua's voice was breathy from his mad dash after me.

"I cannot accept your offer. I am sorry, Joshua." Tears created a new knot in my throat.

My favorite blanket and pillow went into the sack next, and I handled the wooden toys my sire had created for me. My young would surely appreciate them, and I couldn't be sure my sire and dam would accept my decisions and remain in my life. These toys might be all I had left of them, once I fled.

"I don't understand. Why would you leave?"

I didn't reply. To be honest, I wasn't sure I *could* reply with more than a rush of tears. I was leaving the den I'd inhabited my entire life, the personal den I'd shared with my sisters as pups. Facing an uncertain future, I was leaving everything known behind.

I dropped the toys in the sack, my heart heavy.

"Kole?" Joshua asked. "The sire is—"

"Yes. He is. And now you know why I have to leave." I choked out the last few words and pulled the sack shut, tears misting my eyes.

He took my hand and turned me toward him, shaking his head. "No. I don't see."

"*He* doesn't want me, but—"

"I think *I* should be the judge of that," Kole warned.

I turned to look at him, all my hopes disintegrating into nothingness. *Too slow. I shouldn't have taken time to explain to Joshua. I could have been gone before Kole reached me.*

Kole glared at Joshua, but the stubborn buck didn't back down. I pulled lightly at Joshua's grip, and he released me.

Good thing. Kole could slice and dice three of Joshua. When he made his offer, Joshua hadn't known who he would have to fight, and I'd been a fool to believe he'd win such a battle. It had been selfish of me not to warn him what was coming.

Who am I kidding? I thought Kole simply wouldn't want to fight for me. But he will fight for his heirs. I should have known that.

Fury loosed my tongue. "I don't want *you*, Kole. And you are no judge of that." I hefted the sack onto my shoulder and started toward the opening into the larger den.

Joshua took my hand again, and Kole pounced. The smaller buck had just enough time to release me before he was driven back into the den wall. They shoved back and forth, neither shifting to make the fight more serious than it already was. In moments, Joshua was pinned to the wall.

"She is mine, and you would do well to keep your paws to yourself, old man," Kole warned.

"Jellica says you do not speak for her," Joshua replied simply.

"Neither of you speak for me," I retorted. "Both of you would do well to remember that." They might be bucks, but I was a bearing female, and no one crosses a bearing female without scars to show for it.

Two heads swiveled my way, shooting me twin looks of disbelief.

"Out! Both of you... Out of my den." I intended to abandon it within the hour, but for now, it was still mine. Not even the pack Tragen had leave to impose on a denning female. Not even a Keif presumed so much.

Kole pushed Joshua hard against the wall again and stalked toward me. I almost stepped back in fear, but anger won out, and I raised my chin in challenge. He stopped close enough that I could feel his breath bathing my face.

I hated him. There was no denying it. Still, the biological call of mate to mate caused my nipples to harden and my slit to wet at his proximity.

"Out," I repeated, but with less conviction than the last time.

"Jellica." There was no warning in that, but what emotion drove it, I couldn't name.

"You left me, and you have no right to be here."

"My mark—"

"Is nothing. You left it in anger and lust. And then you left *me*. That severs all ties you think you've forged between us."

"I am alpha now. I say what is forged or severed."

"Not if the Tragen disagrees."

Anger poured off Kole in waves. "You intend to ask for that?"

"I have every right to. Why would I want to remain tethered to you?" Just looking at him reminded me there were dozens of reasons I didn't want to admit to. Even before mating called us together, I had admired Kole's body, his reported prowess with women, his proven prowess in the hunt.

He raised one hand and combed his fingers through his fur, stretching his shirt over sculpted muscles.

Dark, thick Fur. Fur that felt so good against my body. A body that felt so right.

Stop it! A few fleeting moments of pleasure aren't worth putting up with Kole's shit.

"I was hoping you'd have at least one reason to."

My cheeks flamed at that pronouncement. "It wasn't that good." *I suppose he thinks so as well. There has to be some reason he didn't come back. Was I less pleasurable than his dalliances had been? The jerk!*

His head cocked to one side. "I wasn't exactly patient. I know that. The rush of mating..."

That almost sounded like an apology. Tears pooled in my eyes, spilling over and making tracks down my cheeks. I wiped them away. "I don't care to find out if it can be better between us."

For a long moment, he stood there, staring down at me. The tension was unbearable.

"The time for making things right has long passed," I inserted into the silence.

Kole snorted as if in disgust. "If I thought you would have forgiven me for my actions, I would have been back in this den within the day."

"Then why weren't you?" I challenged, stung that he was trying to blame his absence on me.

"I know you, Jellica. You are proud and strong and hold one hell of a grudge. You are the epitome of an alpha female. I was wrong to walk out of your den, but you wouldn't have let me walk back in without a fight. I knew the only way I would have a chance at working this out with you was if you couldn't place my sire between us to push me away." He scowled. "Now you want to put the Tragen between us. Do I have to best him in battle as well, just to force you to talk to me?"

Forcing my jaw shut took an inordinate amount of concentration. At a loss for words, I pushed him...hard. Kole didn't move, despite the fact that I'd put all of my body weight into my attack.

Before I could attack again, Kole had his arms around me, one drawing my hips to his and the other hand tangling in my fur. His mouth covered mine, catching me with my mouth open to protest.

The claws I'd loosed settled on his shoulders, but I didn't sink them in. My bark of protest died in a whimper of need. Rather than biting down on his invading tongue, I deepened the kiss.

In the distance, I heard movement that indicated Joshua was taking his leave as quietly as possible. Chances were, he'd be long gone from the den by the end of the kiss, just on the off chance that Kole decided to make an example of him.

Kole took his time. He didn't ease away until my claws had retracted and my jeans were sopping with the proof that I did indeed want to know if it could be better between us.

There were no boastful pronouncements that he'd known I'd react the way I had. Good thing, too. I was already preparing a speech about how it was all animal instincts at work. Lie though it might be, it would help me save face.

Kole sighed in what sounded like frustration. "You're already trying to convince yourself that this isn't personal to you, aren't you?"

"How dare you!"

He raised an eyebrow and waited. When I didn't answer, he continued. "Let me guess...You've either convinced yourself that it's some scheme to get my heirs..."

That was enough to make me jerk away from his hold.

Kole didn't release me. "Or you think I'm worried about what the den will think of me if I don't lay claim to you."

"Well, aren't you?" Both possibilities stung, and either was possible.

"Nothing I can do will stop those tongues from wagging. It will be readily apparent that you've been carrying my young before I properly claimed you. I'm sure Joshua only made his move because of it. How many others are whispering now?"

"Making it right fixes that," I pointed out stubbornly.

"Does it?"

Though I didn't want to admit it, Kole was correct about that. He'd carry a black mark for not properly claiming me in the first place, no matter what happened now.

"It doesn't." He worked the sack off my shoulder and dropped it to the floor. "The fact that I jumped off the ledge and tore off after you mid-speech pretty much said it all. As if you running from me in the first place didn't damn me."

I winced at the mental image. The entire den was likely talking about us now. Why hadn't I walked out sedately?

As if that would have been any better.

"So, as I see it..." Kole eased me toward the mattress. "I've made a complete fool out of myself, and I did that for you. It has to count for something. Right?"

I smacked him hard across the face. "Bucks really are animals, aren't they?" I answered.

He smiled in a way that made my body react sexually. "There is a lot to be said for bedding down with a sexual animal."

I don't want to know. But the lie wouldn't simply oblige me and emerge peacefully. Instead, I fumed at him.

Kole's smile faded, and he pushed my fur back from my face. "I could give you all the assurances you need, but I fear you wouldn't believe them yet."

Yet? Fight or flight set in, and my mind screamed at me to run, but I stood there, staring at him dumbly. What in Mother Moon's name was wrong with me?

The fingers stroking at the wetness between my thighs shocked me to motion. Had I been so lost in thought that Kole had moved and caught me unaware?

I recoiled and found Kole's restraining arm was no longer there. I'd been pressed to him of my own accord? Before I could reason my way to an answer, I was falling. Kole moved fast enough to make my head spin, catching me and lowering me to the mattress.

To my surprise, he didn't follow me down. Instead, he perched over me, balanced in a graceful crouch, my forearms enclosed in his huge human paws. My heart thundered out a warning, but I didn't try to escape him.

"So strong," he whispered.

Kole leaned toward me, and I sank to the mattress we never made it to the night he made me his mate. Would things have been different if we had?

Apparently taking my move as agreement, Kole eased over me. His thighs parted mine, and he pressed his hard cock to the heat gathered for him. I shivered in anticipation more than fear.

"It can be good for you, Jellica," he promised.

"Was it for you?" The question was out before I could rein my tongue. *Of course, it wasn't good for him. He wouldn't have left if it was.*

"So good it scared the hell out of me, and I ran like a pup." That sounded sincere. "The moment I scented you, I knew it was over for me. I couldn't deny you were my mate anymore."

That broke the spell, and I hit him again. "Over for you? How reassuring for me to have you think—"

Kole pressed closer to me, and I gasped.

All right, I admit it. His words almost broke the spell.

"Bucks are animals, but they are juvenile animals, at best," he conceded. "I should have mated with you much earlier, before you were in heat. It wasn't the way I wanted to claim you. I apologize for that."

"You didn't want to claim me at all," I reminded him.

"No male does, but most are smart enough to come to a mate earlier. I was too stubborn for either of our good."

His cock nestled so close to me was miring down my mind, wearing down my resistance to the idea of whatever he wanted to prove to me. "And this accomplishes what?"

"I'll let you decide that."

Kole's mouth covered mine, and his body settled over the length of mine. The last time we were together, he'd taken me from behind, what humans euphemistically call "doggy style". I hadn't felt his weight holding me down then. Oh, what I'd missed out on.

His scent surrounded me, more potent than I remembered. No wonder I was so affected by him.

I took advantage of the position to trail my hands over his body. Squelching the self-righteous voice claiming it was my right to touch what was my own was problematic. *Impossible!*

In a daze, I realized Kole had levered his weight up and was opening my shirt. It wasn't until his lips parted from mine that I protested.

His lips returned but not to mine. Instead, he took one of my breasts into the heat of his mouth. I arched up under him, stunned by the depth of sensation. So this was what he felt he should have done for me? It was tempting to concede that this would have made all the difference in the world, but I wasn't ready to concede much of anything to him, besides my curiosity...and by extension, my body to slake that curiosity.

From breast to breast, he tasted and teased. His shirt disappeared, removed while I was lost in pleasure. Overheated, I dragged my own shirt off and tossed it in the general direction of the sack.

Just as I was considering doing the same with my jeans, Kole took the initiative and opened the button and zipper. I couldn't deny I was in a fever to see what would happen next, and I glanced at the bulge behind his jeans.

Kole eased my jeans down my legs, seemingly in no hurry to release the tension building in me. I thought he'd missed the glance, but I was proven wrong when he commented, "Not until you ask for it."

That raised my ire again. "You'll be waiting a long, damn time."

The sadness in his eyes nearly made me feel regretful for saying it.

Kole went back to disrobing me with a sigh. "Most likely."

In moments, I was nude, and he was still half dressed. The combination made me self-conscious. His hands settled on my knees, halting my attempts to close my legs to him.

He moved downward and inward with excruciating care, and I was gasping for breath by the time his tongue stroked the first time. Oh, Mother Moon, but the stories about his prowess with she-wolves were true.

And once he is finished, I am going to kill him for showing any other female such care.

That was as far as my reasoning mind extended. After that, it was a patchwork of sensation. Kole's tongue was rough but undulating. His fur taunted me with promises of other delights I had no name for. His scent reached a potent edge that screamed for my agreement.

My body reached for something nameless, something whispering just outside the range of my hearing. When it crashed over me, starbursts of color replaced my usual acute vision.

This is what humans mean by fireworks. It was sublime.

My throat aching, I suspected I'd screamed...or perhaps shouted, in the midst of that reaction.

Kole knelt between my thighs, his jeans open but not removed. His eyes questioned me. Was I ready to ask him to prove he could make me feel good while he rutted inside me?

I bit my lower lip, torn. My body was conspicuously empty and wanting, but asking him to touch me, after the way he'd treated me, was more than I could bear.

Kole nodded solemnly. "My apology has only begun."

****

It felt as if Kole had played at my body for days, though I knew it hadn't been more than half a night. I had no clue how many crests he'd brought me to. Though he'd been nude for at least three of them, he still awaited my permission.

In truth, withholding it was downright distressing. I wanted Kole with a fierce hunger and no longer cared that I would be admitting the hunger to him. Even if it wasn't pleasing, it would likely ease the need to feel him inside me again.

And here we were, in the aftermath of yet another of my orgasms, his cock leaking fluids, his eyes pleading for my acceptance. I needed without reason, but still the words stuck in my throat. I reached for him, praying to Mother Moon that Kole would take it as the permission it was.

He didn't. His jaw tightened, and he swiveled his head slowly, side to side. Kole eased my hand off his cock and started to lower his head to my breast.

"Please," I whispered.

He stopped short and looked up at me, seemingly shocked. Tears burned at my eyes.

Damn bearing young causing such emotional unbalance.

"Please?" he questioned.

Why couldn't he simply accept that much? Why did I have to say what I wanted to please him? Wasn't this about appeasing *me*?

As if I'd spoken the questions aloud, Kole capitulated. "Are you giving me permission?"

I nodded shakily, and Kole closed his eyes, murmuring thanks to both me and Mother Moon. I was so stunned by his reaction that his move toward me went unnoticed.

His cock slid several finger-widths into my aroused body and then stopped. I grasped at his shoulder, levering myself farther onto him, my grip tightening in pleasure. Kole pushed deeper with a groan.

"You are so good, Jellica."

I wasn't ready to admit how good he was. I wanted everything I'd been denied in his haste.

Kole stroked deep inside me, and my hips rose in response. I sought out his lips, and Kole lifted me farther into his lap. In moments, he was fully sheathed and moving in long, leisurely strokes that shot me toward another release.

"Jellica, what is this I hear about—" My sire's voice choked off, most likely at the sight of me impaled on Kole's cock.

A glance over my shoulder revealed my sire, pale and nervy, staring at what was most likely the healed mating mark on my shoulder. He shifted from foot to foot, his hands fisting, as if he intended to do Kole harm.

"I have questions for you, Kole," he growled. "After, of course."

"After," my mate agreed.

My sire turned on his heel and disappeared into the larger den, and Kole resumed. A moment ago, I would have sworn that the intrusion had killed my arousal, but it reared up in response to Kole's ministrations.

Kole outlasted me, but only by a few strokes. Panting in my mate's arms, heat pooling inside me, I draped myself around Kole.

"Is my apology accepted?"

I nodded sleepily.

"Will you believe my sincerity?" he asked.

Too tired for games, I answered honestly. "Do you promise a repeat of this?"

He chuckled darkly. "Every night you spend in my bed. Can I take you there now?"

I knew what he was asking. Would I allow him to wrap me in my blanket and carry me across the den to his bed, the healed mating mark on display to confirm the rumors?

"If I don't care for your personal den, I am denning here until whelping," I warned him.

"Agreed."

"My blanket is in the sack." After Kole's apology, I knew any prideful show was over for me. It was time to announce publicly that I was a claimed female.

Section Two

Rise of the Keif

Chapter One

"What's the emergency?" Jen Verik asked, shifting the bag of case files on her shoulder. It was only seven in the morning on a Saturday. If there *wasn't* an emergency, someone's ass was going to fry.

Cal Sanders carded into the security ward of the hospital, and Jen hesitated before following in his wake. Typically, they went to the pediatric ward, two floors up and the opposite direction.

"Security, Cal? Am I seeing a parent first?" That made no sense. She nearly always saw the child first and then talked to a parent.

He jerked a startled look at her. "No." But he offered neither one of his usual quips nor an explanation.

"I'm not juvie, Cal. If this kid—"

"He didn't. Whoever did..." The big man shuddered hard enough to make his unkempt, lightly salt and pepper hair shimmy. "They're sick, Jen, and I won't risk them coming back for the kid."

Jen's mouth went dry at the warning. "How bad is it?" The battered ones always broke her heart.

Cal stopped, took a calming breath, and waved Jen toward a bank of visitor chairs along the wall. When they were seated, he stared off into the distance, seemingly searching for words.

The little details sank in slowly. Cal was pale, unshaven, and decidedly rumpled. It looked like he'd been dragged out of bed.

"Cal?" she prompted him gently.

I don't want to know. I don't need to know.

Remember the kid. There was a reason she still did this job after all she'd seen. There were kids in need, and she was more than willing to advocate for them when no one else would.

"The parents—we *assume* they were the parents—were ripped to shreds. We think the guys used dogs and...and God only knows what else."

"The kid saw it?"

Cal hesitated. "We don't know what he saw yet."

"Is he not talking?" Trauma often made kids retreat.

"He's unconscious. Has been since we found him."

"For how long? How bad is it?" Jen's heart raced. Had the boy been mauled? Physically scarred? Lost body parts? What was she dealing with?

"We're not sure. Forensics figures the parents have been dead for several days. Two. Maybe three. We'll have a better idea once they get time to study the bodies."

Jen's morning coffee fought for escape. "Oh damn."

"The kid doesn't seem to be in bad shape, all things considered. He was covered in blood, mostly his own, but there aren't many cuts. He may have had a bloody nose or— We don't know. The guys didn't even realize he was alive until he flinched when they touched him."

"You're rambling."

Cal nodded. "He has a few small fractures...two on the skull. A lot of bruises. They figure the guys stomping him eased off on the kicks. Maybe had second thoughts about killing a kid."

Words failed her. Jen watched a nurse passing by with a cart of IV bags and meds. The young blond showed her ID to the uniformed officer at the door to one of the rooms, then went inside. The officer looked up and nodded to Cal.

He's in that room. Jen opened her mouth to ask how old they thought the boy was.

The scream from inside the room was high-pitched and broadcasted stark terror. Crashes and shouts overlapped with it.

The next coherent moment for Jen was sprinting down the hall, shoulder-to-shoulder with Cal. The uniformed officer bolted into the room. The child's screams reached a piercing high, and more clashes and clangs followed. Cal wrenched the slowly-closing door open, and Jen ducked through it before he could.

She pushed past the nurse and officer, both of whom were trying to reason with the screaming child. Jen waved them away. They silenced, but they didn't leave the room. Huddled in the far corner of the room, the terrified child carried on with his shrieking, his wide eyes focusing on one person after another.

Jen dropped to her knees and made calming motions. "Shh. Shh. It's okay. You're safe here."

His breathing hitched. His golden gaze panned the room, and the screeching started again.

"Cal, get everyone out."

"But—"

"Trust me. All of you. Out."

He grumbled something Jen didn't catch, and the exodus began. When the door closed behind them, she tried calming the child again.

The hysterics tapered off slowly, and he stared at Jen with red-rimmed eyes, his narrow chest moving in jerking ins and outs. Strands of golden hair jutted from beneath the bandage on his head.

Jen settled cross-legged on the floor, evaluating what she could see of him.

If she had to guess—*and I might*—he was about five years old. Bruises marred his face and arms, a brilliant display of purple, yellow, and green. His right arm was immobilized in a Navy blue brace.

His golden eyes shifted, taking in his surroundings.

"You're at the hospital," Jen whispered. "You're safe. Do you understand?"

A slight nod was his only answer.

"My name is Jen. Can you tell me your name?"

If his expression was any indication, he couldn't remember it. Jen opened her mouth to reassure him that was okay, and he spoke.

"Keif."

She let out a wavering breath. "Keith." *He has a speech impediment. That might help us identify him.*

"Keif," he insisted. "My *name* is Keif."

Odd, but I've heard odder than that. "Good, Keif. Now... Can you tell me your last name?"

The blank expression returned.

Ride it out. Give him time.

"Last...name?"

"Family name? Surname?"

He swiveled his head in a negative response.

"That's okay. You have a head injury. It will come in time."

One small hand crept to the bandage on his head.

"What are your parents' names?" she asked. She had to use the present tense. If he didn't remember their deaths, Jen didn't want to shock him with the truth. *With luck, he has living relatives. Hopefully ones who give a damn about him.*

Figure the odds. It seemed no kid she was called for had that.

"P-parents?"

"Your mother and father? Keif, can you—"

"Mother? Father?"

Good God! How bad is the head injury?

Forget that. "Can we get you back into bed, Keif?"

He looked at the hospital bed and pushed further into the corner, his breathing going ragged.

He's afraid of the bed. They must have attacked him in bed. "Okay. No bed. What about the chair?" Jen tipped her head toward the lounge and attached footstool in the other exterior corner of the room.

Keif surveyed it, then scrambled to it and climbed onto the blue vinyl. He folded his bruised legs beneath the hospital Johnny.

"Pillow and blanket?" she offered.

The boy's gaze focused on the bed. "Yes." It was said with a wealth of longing.

Jen rose slowly, retrieved them, and tucked Keif in on the chair. "Let me see what I can do about getting you something to eat and drink."

Keif hesitated, then nodded. He scratched at the bruise under one eye.

"The people here won't hurt you, Keif. I promise."

He pulled the blanket up to his chin. "Okay."

"They have to run tests to make sure you're not seriously hurt." *Who am I kidding? He is.* "Is that okay with you?"

"Will you be here, Jen?"

"I will. I promise. I have to go to the hall now, but I'll be right back."

He nodded solemnly.

Urgency driving her, Jen went to the hall.

Cal and the uniformed officer looked past her, questions in their eyes.

Jen launched in. "His name is Keif. Not Keith. Keif. No last name he can remember right now.

"We need comprehensive tests. Psych and medical. Keif knows what a bed is...pillow, blanket...but not parents, mother, father. I need to know whether that's emotional trauma or physical injury selectively affecting him. Or abuse. I can't rule out abuse."

Cal nodded. "Anything else?"

"Whatever food they'll allow him. Oh...and no one suggests Keif get into bed."

His jaw tightened down a notch. "Got it."

Chapter Two

Two days later

"Jen? Got a minute?" Dr. Warren asked.

"Sure." She nodded to Keif and the nurse, then accompanied Warren to the hall. Two doors down, he waved Jen into an empty patient room.

It wasn't just Warren waiting for her inside. Reynolds from neurology sat shoulder-to-shoulder with Patterson from developmental peds and Brae from child psychology.

Warren closed the door behind her.

"Team meeting?" Jen asked.

The doctors shot unreadable looks at each other that had snakes writhing in Jen's stomach.

Patterson cleared her throat. "Sort of. You see...none of what we're seeing lines up or makes sense."

Jen settled in an open chair. "In what way?"

Warren lowered himself into the last open chair. "Keif's age, for one thing."

"You're saying you have no idea how old Keif is?"

"Exactly," Reynolds inserted.

"I don't understand." How hard could it be for a group this diverse to come up with an age for a child?

Patterson leaned forward, planting her elbows on her knees. "Based on his size, we all went into this assuming Keif was five, six, maybe seven years old."

"But he's not," Jen guessed.

"Social development is whacked, thanks to what happened to him."

"We think," Brae corrected. "There are just too many holes in his memories to accurately state that."

"Yes. We *think*. Anyway... Language is fairly advanced, despite the holes in family attachments. Maybe eight or ten years, taking those holes into account. Motor skills would indicate a teen or an advanced twelve. I'd speculate he's a young gymnast, but cognitive places him at about ten, as well."

The door opened, and Cal slipped in.

"So...a conservative ten?" Jen asked.

Reynolds spoke up at last. "Dentition says more than twelve. The twelve-year-old molars have all erupted and come into place. That's damned odd for a ten year old."

"He's awfully small for ten, let alone twelve. Does he have a bone growth problem?"

Warren shook her head. "No markers for it on the x-rays or blood tests."

"He was a twin," Cal informed them. "At least...we think he was."

Jen turned to look at him. "What?"

"We found bone fragments that didn't belong to the parents when we were...sifting through." He shifted uncomfortably. "The reason Keif was covered in his own blood but didn't seem to have many injuries was that it *wasn't* all his own."

"Identical twins?" Brae asked.

Cal leaned a shoulder against the wall. "Lab results pending...we believe so."

Warren cut in. "Similar build to Keif's?"

"There aren't enough pieces to speculate on that yet."

Jen's stomach rebelled. "But... The parents... They were torn apart, but there was enough left to work with."

Cal didn't answer. Jen worked at everything she knew about the case.

They used dogs. Oh...shit. They let the dogs eat the boy?

Warren broke the silence. "There's no saying it's a twin then. And at ten or twelve years old, even preemie twins catch up with the growth curve eventually. Usually much earlier than that."

Patterson sighed. "Which leaves us no closer to an answer than we were."

"And running out of secrecy," Cal added. "The press is all over this. We've locked them out for more than two days, and that's a damned miracle."

"We can keep them out of the security wing," Jen noted.

"And refuse to release names, pending notification of next of kin," Warren added.

"That will win us a few more days," Cal agreed. "But little pieces will start leaking out soon. It always happens in a high profile case like this one."

Jen took a calming breath. "Then let's get to work. Dust off your 'no comment', Cal."

35

Chapter Three

Adrien Tragen raped the pot for that first cup of morning coffee. Though his sire claimed it dulled the senses, Adrien had never found that to be true. The heat singed a pleasant trail down his throat, through his chest, and out to his extremities, and he smiled.

He grasped the remote with his free hand and turned on the local news. Then he stretched out on the couch and crossed one bare leg over the other.

The news started out with the usual stories—politics, the search for a murderer or group of murderers—

Using dogs.

Adrien set his mug down on the coffee table and turned the sound up. The story was grim. In the end, he turned the television off and sat brooding.

"Dogs," he grumbled. "Three dead. Rumors of a survivor. Fuck. They're going to find it's wolves. Not dogs. Anyone want to take a bet on that?" he offered to the empty room.

Like it or not, Adrien had to investigate. Chances were, he'd soon be called on to kill someone for this. The bitter slick in his mouth soured him on the idea of finishing his coffee, and Adrien headed for the shower.

****

Finding the site wasn't difficult. Even without the activity buzzing around, the stench assaulted Adrien's senses from a block away.

Saying he snuck past the police would be too crude a term for it. Adrien glided past them, silent and unseen.

The remains had been removed days earlier, he guessed. Not that Adrien needed them. It took only moments to decipher what had happened and moments more to slip back out of the building.

Blocks away and moving fast, Adrien pulled out his cell phone and hit the speed dial for Tragen. His sire answered on the second ring with a grunt that announced his displeasure.

He must have had a late hunt last night. "We have a situation," Adrien informed him.

"Can it be quieted?"

"Too late for that. It's on the news. There was no subtlety about this."

Muttered curses and growls were his sire's only replies.

"I'll call you when it's done," Adrien promised.

"Send a message," the old man ordered. "Send a message that no wolf endangers the pack."

"With your personal regards."

"Which den are we losing pack members from?" It wasn't that Tragen cared. It was a simple calculation. Any wolves who endangered the pack were as good as carrion.

"Not sure yet. The stench of death is overpowering intelligent mark." Adrien shifted the phone and dug the keys to his motorcycle out of his pocket.

"How do you intend to proceed?"

Adrien bristled at having his methods questioned, though it was within his sire's rights to ask it. As the hand of Tragen, Tragen had to be well represented. "There are rumors of a survivor. It won't take me long to get someone to make a move."

"The one who moves in haste—"

"Loses the battle," Adrien finished along with him.

"Good hunting." His sire didn't wait for an answer. The phone clicked.

Adrien shoved the phone in his pocket and swung his leg over his motorcycle.

The pang of disappointment stung. No matter how he reasoned that his sire was just an old wolf set in his ways, it always made Adrien feel dismissed to be cut off that way.

****

At the sight of the news trucks in the hospital parking lot, Jen slipped her ID card into her front pocket. If the reporters caught sight of it, she'd be swarmed, on the off chance that she had information. The vague rumor of a survivor would be "confirmed by an unnamed source" as a child, though Jen wouldn't have spoken a word. Though there were any number of other cases Jen *might* be at the hospital to attend to, the mob mentality of the rabid press would link her to this one.

A guilty pang assaulted her, and Jen did her best to shake it off. She had been away from Keif longer than she'd intended to be, but a hot bath had been too enticing to pass up. For three days, she'd had nothing but rushed showers in Keif's bathroom. A soak with Epsom salts had been long overdue.

Besides, if there was any problem with Keif, they would have called me.

Jen slipped past the line of reporters, feigning interest in her cell phone to obscure her face. A few might recognize her on sight. To her relief, she remained unnoticed and headed for the elevators.

What drew her attention to the man lounging against the wall was an uncertain thing. It wasn't his body, though he possessed a delicious form, topped with shaggy, light brown hair. It wasn't the worn jeans hugging his thighs, black leather boots and jacket, or the skin-tight T-shirt that outlined his sculpted abs.

Jen slowed, staring at him as she passed by.

He's staring at me. No doubt that had caught her attention first.

His unwavering gaze disconcerted her, though she couldn't see his eyes through the dark sunglasses perched on his face. Still, she knew he was focused on her.

His head turned to follow her as she ducked around his position, giving him a wide berth. Hers did likewise, tracking him as he was tracking her.

He flowed leisurely away from the wall and followed her. Jen's heart skipped a beat at the confirmation that he was watching her. For a split-second, she considered going back to the desk and calling Cal from there.

No. If he's following me, he's going to run right into Cal's men...if I let him do it. If I go back, I may be letting a killer escape.

Jen reached for the call button, but his hand was there first.

"Let me." His voice was a low rumble that stirred butterflies in her stomach.

Jen didn't reply to him.

They entered the elevator in silence. Again, Jen considered misleading him. *The vet ward is on six. They're a handy bunch in a pinch. I won't lead him to Keif that way.*

Better to lead him to the police. I can't put more civilians at risk, no matter how much some of them might enjoy the action. She pressed three.

Jen forced herself to look at him. "Which floor?" *That sounded almost normal.*

One side of his lips quirked up. "I'm good."

I'm not.

But it was too late. The doors slid shut, closing them in together.

He didn't waste time. "Are you NPD?"

The elevator hasn't even started moving yet. "No. Why would you think that?"

The lurch beneath her feet announced they were in motion. The clock was ticking.

"Child Services then," he guessed.

Her heart stuttered. In a hospital full of nurses and doctors, patients and visitors, he assumed she was official. How could he know that? "Should I ask who *you* are?" It came out forceful, though her knees were shaking.

He cracked a smile. "Tell me about the boy."

"What boy?" she bluffed.

"I know about the boy. Your jacket reeks of him."

Oh God! He's a psycho, and I'm trapped in an elevator with him. Jen shifted her gaze to the display. *Still a floor to go. Damn hospital elevators for being so slow.*

"You don't have to be afraid of me," he offered in a voice that passed for courteous.

I'll choose who to be afraid of, thanks.

"Believe it or not, we have the same goal."

"I doubt that." The challenge was out before she could rein her tongue. *Too much of Dad in me.*

He leaned toward her, planting one hand on the wall beside her head, invading Jen's space.

"You have spent considerable time with the young one," he stated confidently. "Since he wouldn't be comfortable snuggling with you, you must have spent hours or even days in his company to pick up so much of his scent."

The bell clanged, the floor shifted, and the doors started to open. Jen slid through them before they were wide enough for him to fit through, the bag of fresh clothes held to her ribs so it wouldn't catch.

She hurried toward the guard at the door to the security ward, blessing Cal for assigning one outside the ward once the story broke. A glance back showed her pursuer was in no hurry. He strolled after her, looking amused despite the officer's presence.

The officer in question stepped away from the wall and placed a hand on the butt of his weapon.

Taking the peace bond off.

"Is there a problem here?" he asked.

Jen managed a shaky nod, then took her place behind him. She watched her stalker, waiting for the eruption of violence from him.

This was the safest route. The officer was armed; Jen wasn't. At the same time, Jen had a pass card and the ability to set off the alarms; her protector could only set off alarms. It was a good system. No one could overpower him to get through the door.

But it really wasn't designed for both of us to be in the same place when attack came. I should have led him astray instead of coming this way.

"What is your business here, sir?"

The man in question stopped a little more than an arm's length away. "I need to speak with the officer in charge."

"And who should I say is asking to speak with him?" It was clear he thought whatever the answer was wouldn't warrant calling Cal in.

42

"Tell him Tragen's Enforcer is here. I've come to see the boy."

Tragen's Enforcer? What is that?

The officer took an involuntary step back, colliding with Jen. "If you'd care to wait, I'll call him, sir."

Her stalker smiled, revealing sharpened canines.

Jen's blood ran cold. She'd heard stories about the local pack, but she'd never seen one of their kind before.

That I know of. Who knew a werewolf could look so human?

Chapter Four

Adrien sat in the conference room they'd shown him to, stewing at being left waiting so long. He didn't show it, of course. One never let an adversary know when they were affecting you emotionally. To the humans, he would appear to be lounging, relaxed, his guard down.

The two uniformed officers seemed to be buying it. The woman from Child Services wasn't. Her assessment hadn't eased in more than an hour.

Her tenacity impressed him. She was an alluring mix of grit and arousal that would make any unmated wolf stand up and take notice. A mixture of chase and challenge that fired his libido to life.

Her soft, feminine curves, deep blue eyes, and gleaming black fur didn't hurt either. Yes, she was a woman he could see himself indulging with. A glance at her left hand revealed she hadn't been claimed by another. That meant she was available.

The child and murderers first.

She didn't question Adrien, though she clearly wanted to do so. Instead, she sat, primed to pounce on him.

What a delectable thought.

Any self-recrimination or further investigation Adrien might have made was interrupted by the door opening. The detective rounding it projected an air of alpha male that set off warning bells.

Stifling the urge to establish an order of precedence, Adrien eased to his feet as if he knew he was the highest ranking male in the room. He tipped his head to the detective, ignoring the lesser officers filing into the hall.

"I understand you're Tragen," the other man stated.

"Tragen's Enforcer," Adrien corrected him. If the detective knew anything, he would know Tragen rarely—if ever—interacted with humans. That was left to the Enforcer.

"What *is* an Enforcer?" the woman launched into her questioning.

Adrien let the detective answer for him. In actuality, he wanted to know what the human thought of him, and the words he chose would say a lot about his personal biases or lack of them.

"He's the Tragen's—the pack leader's—police force. The Enforcer handles crimes committed by wolves and against wolves, though our people do *not* always agree with his determinations about the latter. Usually, it's a son or nephew of the Tragen?" His raised eyebrow posed the question of how Adrien was related to the Tragen.

"His son," Adrien confirmed. "Tragen's Enforcer is more than the police. I am also judge, jury, and executioner for those who endanger the pack, especially our own."

An Enforcer turned humans over to the human authorities, as long as there wasn't a wolf looking for the human's blood. In that case, presenting evidence and a corpse was the most expedient method of resolving the breach of trust.

The hotheaded little female shot to her feet, her dark eyes flashing in fury. "If you think you're going to waltz in here and go after a little boy with broken bones and—"

The detective lunged for her and dragged her behind his body. "Jen! No!"

Adrien marveled at her protective instincts. *And those of the detective. They are both very wolf-like.* "Settle down. We never execute young ones. The worst a pup needs fear from me is a growl and nip in warning."

He shifted his focus to the detective. "And I would *never* attack an innocent and defenseless female."

"Never assume Verik is defenseless," the detective warned him in return.

A smile flirted with Adrien's lips. "I'll remember that."

"Then what *are* you here for?" Verik demanded, pushing her way past her human protector with a glare for both of the males in the room with her.

Jen. A lovely name. The name Verik resonated with Adrien and he decided to search online later for some forgotten knowledge he felt would be of use in dealing with her.

She asked a question. I should answer her before she decides I'm ignoring her. It never served one well to let a female think you were ignoring her. Adrien sighed. "The boy. I need to confirm his identity and find out which wolves did this."

"He can't tell you either of those things. Not completely, anyway."

That surprised him. "You mean he *won't* tell you. Any pup raised in the isolation of a den will be fearful of exposing the pack, even in the case of—"

"Keif is *not* a werewolf," Jen insisted.

Adrien's stomach lurched. "What did you call him?"

"Keif," the detective repeated for her.

Mother Moon! I don't know who did this, but I know why he did.

****

The Enforcer's stillness raised the hair at the base of Jen's skull. "You know Keif," she guessed.

"*The* Keif. Keif isn't a name. It's a title."

"Do you know him? His parents? His last name?" His reactions said he did.

He didn't respond, and what he did say was so low, she almost missed it. "But why would he tell humans that? Why not his name?"

Jen resisted the urge to point out that humans weren't all bad. "Keif has memory loss. He remembers things like the names for objects, math...but not parents, mother, father, last name—"

"Sire and dam. Den affiliation."

"What?"

47

"The Keif would be familiar with the terms sire and dam, not father and mother. He wouldn't consider his den affiliation a name. To him, it would be a place or a group of people. And he might have offered his sire's name instead of his den alpha's name, since that is what we typically use, unless we are dealing with human authorities."

"You're saying I've been asking him the wrong questions?" That was a relief.

"Perhaps." There was something unsaid. Something cautious...

Or something he's hiding from me. "But? There's more."

The Enforcer focused on her. He remained silent for a long moment. "The Keif should have given you his name. Any pup old enough to be...known as a Keif would have enough human language to understand that father and mother are sire and dam."

He hesitated long enough to make Jen's lungs ache. She expelled her breath slowly. The Enforcer sank into the chair he'd vacated, and she did the same. Cal took the chair to her right.

At last, he spoke. "What were the Keif's injuries?"

Jen winced. "The murderers kicked him repeatedly. Stomped was the term I think one of the doctors used for it. They cracked some bones. Hairline—"

"They healed. Trust me. They were broken. Possibly shattered. The wolves who did this wanted to kill him; they thought they had. They wouldn't have left him until they were certain they had."

"Then his skull was originally fractured in at least two places. His arm. He's got severe bruising on his legs, ribs and back but no obvious fractures."

His expression said he wanted to correct her again, but he didn't.

Jen continued. "He could have had much more serious injuries than we originally thought...if you're right that he's one of you."

"I'm correct." It was stated with confidence. The Enforcer didn't elaborate.

"We assumed the memory gaps were trauma-induced. A fugue. They seemed specific to the family he lost. I mean, it's fairly common for a child to repress painful memories, and seeing your parents and brother ripped apart—"

His head snapped around, and he focused the full intensity of his golden gaze on her.

Golden eyes. How did I miss that when he took his sunglasses off? Keif must be one of them after all.

"Brother? Older or younger than the Keif?"

Cal broke in. "There's not enough left of the kid to be sure. The forensic specialists are working on estimating a height from bits and pieces of bone."

"What do you have?"

"Bone fragments. Some tissue. A whole hell of a lot of blood."

The Enforcer leaned across the table. "What *kind* of bones?"

Cal shifted uncomfortably. "Skull and jaw pieces that we're sure of...maybe a portion of the ulna and tibia. It's hard to figure out when they're little pieces."

He nodded but remained silent.

"Enforcer?" Jen prompted him.

"My name is Adrien," he invited. "What are you asking, Jen?"

Cal bristled at his familiarity.

Jen ignored him. "Why did you ask which bones? What does it mean to you?"

"I don't think the Keif had a brother. In fact, I'm fairly sure I'm correct. The bones line up with injuries he has, just as I expected they would."

"Bruises," she countered. "He has bruises and small fractures. He doesn't have gaping wounds."

"Now. The assassins sent for him assumed the Keif hadn't developed his healing yet. They crushed him with their battering and left him for dead. While he could grow back his skull and brain tissue, he can never grow back the memories stored in the lost tissue."

The urge to puke at the mental image rode Jen hard. She swallowed down a sour wave.

The Enforcer didn't seem to notice. "I will have to bait the guilty party to me with little or no information from the Keif to aid me."

"And if you can't bait them?" Jen asked.

"The Keif will remain in my care...my personal protection, until his attackers are punished or he reaches adulthood."

"That long?"

He turned his head and focused on her. "We mature faster than humans do."

"That might explain the conflicting test results," Cal inserted himself into the conversation again.

"Probably so," the Enforcer agreed.

Jen seized the opportunity to end the speculation. "He's the size of the average human five year old, but Keif has skills that range from those of an eight year old to a twelve year old and the teeth of a twelve year old. How old would you estimate he is?"

He hesitated. "I would have to see the Keif to be certain. The kind of healing required would indicate at least nine years, but the rest...perhaps...five years old. He would be exceedingly small to appear so young at nine." His brow furrowed in seeming confusion. "I have never heard of fully realized healing at younger than eight...nor of a Keif displaying his abilities at younger than seven. At any rate, he will grow into his bulk quickly once he reaches ten years and be fully adult by fifteen or sixteen."

The mental math floored her. "You're prepared to take on Keif's care and protection for the next decade?"

His expression didn't falter. "If that is necessary, I will make myself ready."

Jen's cheeks heated, and she swallowed what she suspected was a sob rising in her throat. *If only human men were so responsible.*

****

Something in Jen's expression made Adrien want to soothe her pain.

Not now. "I have to make a call. After that, I will see the Keif."

He didn't make it a question. By the Human-Were Pact, they could not refuse Tragen's Enforcer or Tragen himself access to any wolf—adult or pup—in human care or custody.

Jen shot a pained look at the detective. "Can I be there, Cal?"

He motioned to Adrien. "That is up to the Enforcer. I cannot force that on him."

She met Adrien's eyes but didn't repeat the question.

He nodded. "The Keif clearly trusts you. If he has no memory of den and pack, he may require something familiar."

Jen seemed surprised by the response, but she didn't say why she was.

Adrien rose. "Five minutes." He strode into the corridor, then to the window and the likelihood of a clear signal for his cell.

His sire answered on the first ring, indicating that he'd been waiting for an update. His snarled greeting belied that.

"Has the discovery of a Keif been reported to you?" Adrien inquired. *The Keif should have been. Immediately.* That meant Tragen should know the Keif's name and den affiliation. It would be the best place to start an investigation, since the denmates anticipating leadership would have the most to lose by the appearance of a Keif.

"What? No. Where did you hear such a thing? Is it substantiated?"

That got the old buck's attention. Something about his sire's reply bothered Adrien, but he couldn't name what with certainty.

"It is an unsubstantiated rumor." *So far. I will know the truth soon.* "Just eliminating the possibility."

"You know I would have told you if a Keif had been identified."

Some wouldn't. But was his sire the guilty party? Was someone in Adrien's den? Or someone in the Keif's den? On closer inspection, his own den had even more to lose than the Keif's den did.

"Of course. I just had to be sure before I dismissed the possibility."

"Is there a survivor?" Tragen changed the subject.

I shouldn't confirm it. Not while Tragen is a suspect. "Also unsubstantiated, at this point." *I've only established that there is a pup here.* "I have just established an agreement with the human authorities on the case and started to gather what information they have. You know how long that takes."

"Nothing more?"

"I have established that the killers and the dead are ours."

"Three dead?" There was an edge of something fierce in that.

Again, Adrien hesitated to tell his sire what he knew to be true. "The human police have the remains of three, I am told. Male, female, and male child." *I'm not lying to him.*

I am misleading my sire. My Tragen.

Only until I know Tragen isn't involved. It is my duty to safeguard both the pack and the Keif.

The Keif is the future of the pack.

There was a potent moment of silence. "Keep me informed, Adrien."

"I will."

The click ended their discussion. Adrien closed the phone, pushed it deep into his pocket, and turned away from the window.

Jen watched him from the security door. "Detective Cal" stood at her shoulder, dwarfing her.

Protecting her. Does he believe he has a claim on Jen? Adrien didn't question that Jen hadn't accepted such a claim.

"Ready?" Cal asked.

Clearly trying to speed me away. Adrien nodded.

That time, the uniformed officer didn't block the door. Jen and Cal passed through, and Adrien followed. There was another uniformed officer at the far end of the hall, leaving no doubt as to the Keif's whereabouts.

Sloppy. A pack member could be to the Keif in heartbeats.

"Is there a problem, Adrien?" His name rolled off her tongue as if Jen was testing the taste of it.

"What makes you say that?" Humans couldn't usually read him that well.

"You're tense. Just like you were when you were waiting for Cal to show up."

Amazing. "Since you asked, yes. This entire setup is inadequate. If the Keif's condition will allow it, I'll have to move him. Soon. Tomorrow at the latest. Today would be safer."

Cal stopped short a body length from the Keif's door and shot Adrien a sour look. "Inadequate?" he challenged.

"To stop one of my kind? Let alone several of them? Absolutely."

Jen stepped between them. "Enough. Both of you. If Keif isn't safe here, he has to be where he *is* safe."

Her answer surprised Adrien. He'd expected her to balk at the idea of the Keif leaving the hospital. It pleased him to hear her putting the pup's safety first. He could easily see her as dam to a very lucky young one.

"Indeed," he agreed. With that, Adrien pushed through the door the uniformed officer stepped away from.

He'd barely had a chance to focus on the pup when the blow to his chest sent Adrien reeling. He landed hard on his knees, marveling at the Keif's mastery in attack. He'd believed, until that moment, it had been pure luck the child had survived. Adrien was no longer certain of it.

A blur of woman shot past him, and Adrien reached for Jen, his heart pounding. She slipped through his fingers, and Adrien started to shout a warning. Approaching a frightened, lawless pup was a disaster in the making.

"Keif, no!" Jen let out a frightened little scream as the Keif grasped her arm and wrenched her behind his slim body. Her feet slipped from under her, and she thumped to the floor with a huff of expelled air from her lungs.

The pup rose from a crouch, the hospital Johnny swaying around his pajama-clad legs. His bare feet were planted shoulder-width apart on the tile floor, and he looked ready to battle anyone who came his direction.

It's a damned miracle Jen hasn't been killed accidentally already.

The Keif's growl raised the light fur at the back of Adrien's skull and shoulders. The pup continued in the rumblings of pack language.

"Harm her and you will die."

If the situation hadn't been so deadly serious, Adrien would have laughed at the idea of a pup warning him off. As it was, he didn't dare. Not with Jen in the room with them. Adrien ducked his head in a show of subservience, watching for the Keif's reaction through his lashes.

The boy stared at him, seemingly shocked. His trembling became more pronounced, but he didn't back off or relax.

Jen pushed to her knees behind the child. "He's here to protect you, Keif. Calm down."

The growl that followed left no doubt the pup saw Adrien as an enemy.

Is it the pack scent? Or is it the scent of my den? Adrien wanted to believe it was the former, that the child was simply confused. The alternative meant Adrien was hunting his own den.

He spoke slowly and in English, trying to draw the pup back to the child Jen knew. "I am Tragen's Enforcer. Do you remember what that means, pup?"

The Keif's brow furrowed. "Tragen is..." His gaze shifted toward Cal, then snapped back to Adrien. "Boss."

"Yes. Tragen is the pack leader." *For now.* "He protects all pack members." *I hope to Mother Moon Tragen isn't guilty.* "I am Tragen's Enforcer. I protect you for Tragen, and I will kill those responsible for what happened to you and your sire and dam."

"Jen will protect me," he insisted. "Jen stays with me. I stay with Jen." It sounded like he was issuing an ultimatum.

Or repeating something he has foreseen. Was that how they knew he was a Keif? Did the child start seeing the future? At this age? He can't be more than six...if that.

I should find out which it is. "How do you know Jen will protect you?"

"I know. I...saw her."

His throat went dry at the pronouncement. "What did you see? When did you?"

The Keif's eyes went momentarily unfocused. "I saw her in the dark and cold. Before I came here. In the bad-smell place. The place full of pain. I saw...Jen's...green place. She will keep me safe there. Her apartment is too small, but her green place is big enough..." He snapped a look at Adrien that said he didn't like talking to him.

"Green place? My... How could you know that, Keif?" Jen questioned. "And how could you know my apartment is small? How do you even know I live in an apartment?"

Adrien waved her off. "Was I at the green place? Think hard, my Keif. Was I there?"

The pup bared his teeth, letting Adrien see them lengthen and sharpen. "I don't *need* you."

"I believe you. But...was I there?" Adrien needed his agreement to protect the Keif properly.

The pup turned his head to look at Jen, then swiveled his gaze back to Adrien again. "Jen may need you," he conceded. "Jen protects me, but I cannot protect her alone. You may stay with me, Enforcer. For Jen."

Adrien let out a slow breath. He glanced up at Jen. "Where is your green place?"

"How does Keif even know about that?" Her face was red in what he would assume was frustration.

"The Keif sees future events. For him, the future is fact. We will all be at that place together."

"I haven't agreed to take you there," she protested.

The Keif looked at her, his eyes pleading. "You want to leave me, Jen?"

She hesitated, then reached out to pull him into her arms. "No, Keif. If you need me, I'll be there for you. You know that."

His little arms circled her neck. "I do know it."

Adrien didn't doubt that was true. The Keif knew absolutely that Jen would stay with him. For the pup, it was infallible.

"We should go tonight, Jen. Definitely tonight."

She looked up and met Adrien's gaze, clearly startled. "Should we go sooner? This afternoon?"

The Keif was silent for a long moment. "Sooner is better. Sooner is good."

Adrien leapt to his feet, sending Cal shuffling away from him. "Give me thirty minutes to switch vehicles. Can you be ready that soon?"

"Clothes for Keif?" Jen countered. "We can't take him out of here in the Johnny. It will attract too much attention."

He nodded solemnly and sized up the pup again. "An hour."

****

"Turn here." Jen pointed to a dirt track that was nearly covered in encroaching plants.

Adrien turned onto it, taking the time to appreciate the term the Keif had used for it. *Green place.* They were well outside the city, moving from paved roads to gravel to dirt roads with no signs. This place was nothing if not green. His wolf ached for a run at the sight of it.

In the back seat, the Keif sat, looking out the window, his attention fixed on the passing scenery. He wore a child-sized version of the same sunglasses Adrien did and an adult's ball cap to cover his still-healing head wounds.

Adrien had misjudged the pup's shoe size by a full size, and the too-large tennis shoes were on the floor of his car. The clothes fit well, thankfully. On one of his outings to get information, Adrien could easily replace the shoes, though most pups preferred to go barefoot, even in human form. It would have been more time-consuming to replace the clothing as well.

And it would have been conspicuous if the boy's clothes hadn't fit properly.

Leaving the hospital had proven painless. With the Keif's permission to let Adrien carry him, they'd simply walked past the reporters, blending in as an ordinary couple with a child. No one had looked twice.

Now they were nearly fifty miles away. "How much further?" he asked.

Jen pointed to the top of the hill rising before them. "Just on the other side of the hill. There's a lake back there. Only a few cabins scattered around it, and not many people come up here once it starts cooling off."

"Is the house heated?" He wasn't worried about himself or the Keif. They would survive a few cold nights well enough. *But Jen is human.*

"There's a wood burning stove. I don't know how much wood is stocked for it, though. I haven't been up here for more than a year."

Adrien smiled. "I'm handy enough with an axe. There will be wood for us."

She nodded. "If you check on the wood, I'll start up the generator and check the propane level for the stove."

"I'll do that. Just get the Keif settled—"

"Keif," the pup insisted. "Not *the* Keif."

Jen's voice overlapped with his. "I am more than capable of—"

"Okay," Adrien conceded. He wasn't sure which one he was trying to placate, but both seemed like a good idea.

For the moment. Eventually, I have to get the Keif to accept his true name. Of course, there was no point in that until he knew what name to introduce the pup to.

He pulled the car to a stop in the clearing next to the cabin and parked it. Before he was fully out of the vehicle, the Keif was out and heading for the porch at a run.

"Keif! Wait!" Jen called after him.

Adrien shook his head. "He will be safe. He knows he's safe here."

"It's locked. He can't get in without me." She raised keys in one hand.

They rounded the cabin together.

Proving Jen wrong, the Keif had retrieved a key from some hiding place that was not readily apparent to Adrien and was busy unlocking the door. In a matter of heartbeats, he was inside, his small feet pounding over hard wood floors. From the sounds of it, he went directly to where he wanted to be and stopped there.

Jen stood, her gaze focused on the porch roof, her mouth hanging agape.

"What is it?" Adrien asked.

"*I* can't reach that."

Adrien chuckled and led the way inside. If Jen expected the Keif to have the physical abilities of a human child of the same age, she was in for something of a surprise.

Jen started checking the rooms, calling out the Keif's "name". She stopped at the third door, and her brow furrowed. "We should use the other room."

The pup's voice was hard in decision. "This is my room, Jen. I saw it."

"But the bed in the other room is much larger. We can both be comfortable there," she counseled.

"I saw it," he replied stubbornly.

Jen slid a look at Adrien that said she was discomfited. Her meaning was clear. There were only two beds. If she chose to stay in the room with the Keif, she would be uncomfortable sharing the small bed with him, but the only other choice was sharing a bed with Adrien, and she wasn't comfortable with that either.

Adrien opened his mouth to offer to sleep on the floor with the blankets he kept in his trunk for emergencies.

The Keif beat him to the punch. "You will have this bed, Jen. The Enforcer can move my chair for me."

"Your chair?" she questioned him.

"The big one in the last room. That is my chair."

Jen's expression said the pup had been correct, though they both knew he hadn't had time to explore and find the chair in question.

"As my Keif wishes," Adrien agreed. He turned and made his way to the room the Keif had indicated.

It was an office with the faint scent of male. Adrien drew the scent in, relaxing when it proved to be family scent, close to Jen's. A father or brother, he would wager.

There was no question which chair the Keif meant. The only two chairs in the office were a rolling chair behind the desk—hardly a proper bed—and a large overstuffed leather chair. Perfect for a small pup.

Adrien bent down to heft it. He stopped halfway to his feet, his gaze locking on the display of awards given to former military. Next to it was a second one. *A policeman's slate of awards.*

His head spun in realization. *Verik. Jen is the daughter of Andrew Verik.* His uncle had liaised closely with the man while he'd been a police commander and then the chief of police; Adrien had been introduced to the alpha human early in his training.

Before he died. I never had the chance to liaise directly with him, but I wish I had been so honored. Adrien had respected the man. In retrospect, it was easy to see her father's attributes in Jen, both the physical and in personality. The duo were alphas among those who didn't respect alphas as wolves did.

"Enforcer?" the Keif questioned him from the doorway.

He turned with the chair in hand, trying to remember everything he knew about Andrew Verik. His uncle had a nickname for the human, one that demanded attention and respect from any wolf who heard it. "On my way."

The Keif didn't move. He stood in the doorway, forcing Adrien to stop and meet his gaze. "You understand?" he asked. "You understand *who* Jen is?"

"This woman is an ally, the daughter of a formidable ally to the pack. She deserves our greatest respect." It was a guess, but it was a good one.

He nodded, then padded back down the hallway. There, the Keif entered into an animated discussion with Jen.

Jen Verik. The Lion's daughter. The young Lioness.

Chapter Five

"Tragen's Enforcer, Draven," the youth announced.

Adrien strode past him and into Draven's lounging den. This was the third den he'd visited, and there'd been no indication of a home den for the Keif yet.

This den was promising. Though the Keif had a very faint scent of den, Adrien would lay wagers this one was the young leader's birth den.

The den alpha didn't rise to meet him, his careless disregard a cool dismissal of the power Tragen invested in Adrien and of Adrien's own standing. It was a long moment before Draven sent the pups he'd been instructing away and sized up his visitor. The air was potent with musk, and tension sizzled around them.

"What is your purpose here, Enforcer?"

"I am tracking a small unit—male, his mate, and a male pup of perhaps five or six years. They would have been away from home den long enough to lack a strong scent, and they would have been out of contact with home den for close to a week or longer."

His eyebrows rose at that. "Then you don't know who you are tracking. That complicates your...job."

A subtle snub. Adrien ignored it. "I know roughly *where* they are. Who they are will answer questions of affiliations and motives. *Your* den seems a close match for the unit."

Draven's stiffening posture announced that Adrien's search was over. "What are they accused of, Enforcer?"

"Do you know of such a unit?"

The alpha glared at him. "I asked you a question, Enforcer."

"I asked you one as well." This may be Draven's den, but no wolf stood in the way of Tragen's Enforcer performing his duty.

A low growl left Draven's lips, and he showed his teeth. "Dara is innocent. Whatever her bastard of a mate has done, Dara and Michael are innocent of it."

"How long has it been since the unit has contacted you?"

He visibly fumed. "My *daughter,* Enforcer. My *daughter* hasn't contacted me for well over a week. I should have known that bastard—"

"Do you have anything with Dara's scent on it?"

"To check against the scent you already have of them?"

The Keif's scent. He nodded.

Daven stomped away and returned a few minutes later with a cushion pungent in female scent and a blanket that reeked of the Keif.

Adrien didn't take them. He nodded solemnly and launched into his questioning before Draven could question him.

"I take it Dara's mate isn't a loosely-connected member of your den." If he was, Draven would have killed the buck before allowing a wolf he didn't trust to lay claim to Dara.

Draven snorted, his lip curled in disgust. "He's a grandpup of Morgan. He was named for his gran-sire."

Draven's enemy. "A *Romeo and Juliet* situation."

"Morgan allowed Dara to stay when they mated, but it wasn't an easy alliance. Dara refused to den with them and convinced the younger Morgan to come here until Michael's whelping...and then his weaning."

"They were welcome here?"

The fur on Draven's head bristled in warning. "Dara is my daughter. She and hers are always welcome here."

"Then why did they ultimately choose to live with Morgan's—"

"They don't. The younger Morgan's...human interests aren't far from Morgan's den. They live apart from both dens and visit often."

"There were no grudges? On either side?"

Draven's eyes narrowed. "Against one of our own? Even that old jackal Morgan wouldn't attack his own get unprovoked." There was a moment of tense silence. "Has someone harmed my Dara?"

Damn. Adrien had hoped to avoid this longer. As long as Draven didn't know the facts, he would be content to aid Adrien, for Dara's sake. *Once he knows, he'll want blood.*

"Enforcer?" he warned.

There was no way to avoid it. "She's dead, Draven. Tragen sends his assurances that those responsible will die for it."

"I will be sure of it."

That complicated things.

"Where is Michael? With his sire?" he asked urgently.

He probably thinks Morgan's den killed Dara to drive young Morgan and the pup home to them. It was a plausible explanation, but it didn't explain killing the younger Morgan and attempting to kill the boy.

Draven lunged for him, and Adrien side-stepped him.

"Her mate is also dead."

The color seeped from the den alpha's face, and he stumbled a step before he caught himself against the wall.

"The pup lives," Adrien hastened to assure him.

"I claim Michael as get of my den. I demand his return, Enforcer."

"At this time—"

"I will not accept Morgan's claim on my grandpup. I will go to Tragen. He was born in *my* den. It was his dam's wish that—"

"For the time being, the pup is under *my* care. Until we learn the identity of the killers and put them down, the boy will remain safely in my care."

"You think I am incapable of protecting my own den?" Draven challenged.

"I *know* there is every possibility that the killers came from within your den or Morgan's. Until the guilty are dead, the pup will not be placed at risk of a second attack on his person."

Draven motioned wildly toward the inner den. "None of us would—"

"Kill a rival? Especially if the killer is also a young wolf?"

Draven hesitated for a long moment. "I don't understand what you're saying."

"Michael is a Keif. If he reaches maturity, he could demand leadership of either your den or Morgan's, and whichever he chooses must comply."

He didn't argue it. "Are you certain he is a Keif?"

"Beyond any doubt at all. A young wolf with aspirations of leadership and a following... A child of two dens who, at a whim, could choose to take the place the other envisions for himself—"

"And even Tragen would have to bow to Michael."

"I know it. No one is above suspicion, but Tragen has no direct contact with the Keif. Any conspiracy to remove him would have to had come from inside the sire's den or the dam's."

Draven shot a look around, probably making sure they were unheard. "I don't believe Michael will be any safer with Tragen than he would be with me."

"Michael won't *be* with Tragen. He will be with me."

"These wolves have already killed two full-grown wolves. Love him or hate him, I must admit young Morgan was a wolf to be feared in battle."

"Those two wolves didn't know the attack was coming. I do. And I have the Keif directing his own safety. He has already chosen a place his visions say is safe for him."

"Visions? He can't be having visions. Michael won't reach six years until the height of winter. He is too young to display that ability."

Very young to be showing such prowess. "I said there was no doubt," Adrien reminded him.

Draven sighed. He rolled his shoulders. "Keep him safe, Enforcer. I will see what I can find for you."

"Appreciated."

The alpha offered the pillow and blanket. "Take these with you. Michael will find them comforting."

Adrien took them. "I'm sure he'll appreciate them. My thanks. I should go now. I have to talk to the elder Morgan before I return to the Keif's temporary den."

Draven nodded. "Tell Michael... Tell him I miss him."

He hesitated. "I will." There would be time to tell Draven his grandpup might not remember him later. The alpha had suffered enough today.

****

Adrien returned to the cabin late that afternoon, looking weary. The sight of the strong wolf in such a state made Jen's stomach roil.

"Did you learn anything?" she asked.

He dropped two sacks to the floor and sank into the chair at the head of the table. "I've identified the Keif's den affiliations but not the killers...yet."

Jen settled in the chair across from him. "And?"

"The leaders of the dens are innocent. I am certain of it, but I don't doubt the attacks originated from one or both dens." He hesitated. "They are both trying to claim Michael... His name is Michael Morgan."

"You said wolves don't have surnames." He'd explained to her that they found the term *werewolf* a slur after she used it at the hospital.

"It's not a surname. The second name identifies the pup's sire. His sire's name was Morgan."

"Will we have to return him to them soon? If the attack came from inside..." She couldn't wrap her mind around the idea of Keif as a Michael.

"Not at this time. I believe Michael when he says he's safe here. If he believes that, his life may depend on it."

"I will not leave here yet," Keif insisted from the doorway.

Jen offered him a smile. "No one will take you from here, as long as you think we need to be here."

He nodded solemnly, then looked to Adrien. "What is that?" He pointed to the sacks on the floor.

"Belongings I picked up from your sire's home den and your dam's home den. They're yours."

Keif scampered across the room and dropped to sitting next to the sacks. He dug into the first one, pulling out clothing in his size, wooden toys, and a man's leather jacket. None of it seemed to make much of an impression on him.

Adrien started speaking. "The jacket was your sire's. His name was Morgan. His sire, David, died a long time ago, but David's sire, also named Morgan, is alpha of the den."

Keif held the jacket to his nose for a moment, then nodded.

He set it aside and reached into the second sack.

"Your dam's name was Dara. Her sire, Draven, is the alpha of her den. Your name, young Keif, is Michael."

"Keif," he insisted. "I want to be called Keif."

"As you wish, but your name is Michael, and your denmates will invariably call you that."

A plush blue blanket emerged from the sack and Keif wrapped it around his shoulders. A purple pillow that looked like Chenille knit followed. Keif ran a hand over it, hesitated, then raised it to his face, inhaling deeply, his eyes closed.

"Both sides wish to claim you as their own," Adrien informed him. "Your gran-sire Draven and great-gran-sire Morgan both miss you desperately. You will have to choose which den will be your home someday. But not today."

Keif didn't reply to that. He stood and walked toward the bedroom, the pillow held to his cheek, the blanket draped around him and dragging the floor like a train, and the jacket folded sloppily over his arm.

Jen pushed to her feet and followed him, stunned by his silence. She found him in the bedroom, curled up on the chair he'd claimed. The jacket was hung over the head of the chair, the pillow cushioning his cheek, and the blanket cocooning him. His eyes were closed, and he hummed what was surely a lullaby. A tear wound its way down his cheek.

Adrien took her hand and tugged Jen away. "He needs time."

She went along without an argument. Keif clearly wanted to be alone with his fractured memories for a while.

Chapter Six

Jen came half-awake at the shifting of the mattress. It took only a moment for her to identify Keif's body nestling to hers. She shifted, allowing the little boy to snuggle to her shoulder, then wrapped an arm around him.

A smile pulled up at her lips. This was the first time he'd slept in a bed willingly since he'd been found.

At the same time, she found the situation heartbreaking. Someday soon, she would have to return Keif to his family. Living apart from their den or not, wolves had close extended families, and those families had rights...and wishes and feelings.

I'm not a wolf. She couldn't possibly teach a young wolf what he needed to learn. He needed his kind.

He's not my son. Jen had to remember that. As much as she enjoyed being his stand-in mother, it wasn't going to last.

Tears burned at her eyes behind her closed eyelids, and she swallowed a lump in her throat.

Stop it. I knew years ago that this was the way it would be.

Try as she might to banish them, memories flooded her mind, memories of Tyler she'd love to expunge completely. The replay cut off abruptly at the growl rising from Keif.

Jen jerked to sitting, hissing at the burn of scratches on her arm. She tried to focus on the dark mass on the bed with her.

The door, left ajar while they slept, crashed open against the wall. In the light from the kitchen, a huge wolf took shape. Its eyes glowed in the dim light. Its teeth were bared and its hackles raised.

One pissed off wolf. Jen fought for a decent breath, frozen in place by the sight.

Keif's growl deepened, and a large paw settled on the quilt next to Jen's leg. She forced her gaze from the wolf in the doorway to the child at her side.

Calling him a "child" at that instant was a bit of a stretch. Red-gold fur covered his oddly-shaped arms, disappearing beneath his pajama top. His muzzle was drawn back to bare deadly teeth to his rival.

"Calm, my Keif."

Jen snapped her head around at the sound of Adrien's voice. The wolf in the doorway was gone, replaced by the Enforcer.

It was him. Adrien's wolf form.

He'd adopted a pose she could only classify as subservient. His right knee was planted on the floor, his left foot placed beside it.

Ready to move, if necessary. Then again, he'd come to his feet from both knees in one smooth move at the hospital.

Both closed fists were pressed to the hard wood floor, and his head was bowed so deeply Jen could see his shoulders bunching and releasing.

The final realization made her heart race. Adrien was nude.

She reasoned that he probably had to be nude to shift forms, but seeing him like this was a shock nonetheless. Should she look away? Did wolves have any sensibilities about nudity for her to offend?

Keif sank to her side, and she glanced his way, relieved to see he'd shifted to his 'little boy' shape again. He was panting hard and coated in sweat, but he was human again.

The hair standing on end behind his head announced his upset. She stifled the urge to smooth it down. Keif was already primed to attack, and she'd learned he could accidentally hurt her that way. The bruises on her hip were still healing.

Adrien raised his head. "I meant no threat, my Keif. I heard sounds of distress."

His explanation calmed Keif, and the hair relaxed against his head.

"I think he had a nightmare," Jen informed Adrien.

The Enforcer started to nod.

"It *wasn't* a dream," Keif insisted.

Adrien's gaze went hard; his muscles tensed. "Is there danger coming for us?"

Jen opened her mouth to ask what sort of question that was. *He sees the future,* she

76

reminded herself. *Do we have to leave here and find somewhere else?*

"Not yet," Keif assured them. "If I know in time, I will tell you, Enforcer."

Adrien's shoulders eased. "Is there anything else I can help you with?" There was a note of sincere hope in Adrien's voice.

Keif stared at Jen, seemingly assessing her. The intensity of his gaze set her nerves on edge.

At last, the child looked away. "Soon. In the meantime, you should help Jen clean her wounds."

She started to protest that she wasn't hurt, but a glance at her forearm showed blood running lazily down her hand from the scratches.

"I am sorry, Jen. I didn't mean to harm you."

Her move to answer ended on a gasp as Adrien lifted her from the bed and marched toward the kitchen, as if she weighed no more than Keif did.

And he's nude. Adrien was more than just a naked man. He was eye candy of the sweetest sort.

Jen would have liked to say that smacked common sense into her. She'd learned her lesson about eye candy a long time ago.

Common sense was nowhere to be found. *Of course.* It seemed she would never learn.

Adrien deposited her on the chair and turned to retrieve the first aid kit from beneath the sink. She ordered her eyes to find a neutral location, trying not to obsess over the fact that he looked just as good from the back as he did from the front.

****

Adrien placed the first aid kit on the table, then collected a clean washcloth from the drawer. He ran hot water over the fabric and poured soap onto it, then squeezed out the excess liquid.

Jen winced at the first swipe down the length of the wound.

He tried to remember what he'd learned about human physiology, but it escaped him. "I do not believe you require stitches."

She shook her head. "No. Just some antibiotic gel and a bandage."

She is so fragile. Had she been a wolf, it would have been a waste to bandage so small a wound. "How long will it take to heal?"

Jen turned her arm and looked at the cuts, seemingly considering it. "A week or so, I guess. They aren't that deep."

It was hard to conceive of the woman with the grit to shout Adrien down suffering such frailty. A week to heal something he could heal in a few scant hours. How did humans thrive?

"Do you suffer some slowing of your healing?" The question was out before Adrien could rein his tongue.

"No. We just aren't all wolves," she offered acidly.

He pulled the antibiotic gel from the kit and opened it, while he considered how best to mollify her. "I mean no offense," he apologized. "I am afraid I've forgotten much of what I know about human health topics." Adrien smoothed the gel down the cuts, thankful that she didn't wince again.

"Is that a normal topic wolves learn about in...school?"

"No, but those who will be Enforcers must learn about the human world. We also watch news reports...for obvious reasons."

"That makes sense. You have to liaise."

Adrien nodded. "We do." He opened a gauze pad and placed it over the lower end of the cuts, then a second over the upper. He'd wrapped the gauze roll around her arm twice when her expression caught his eye.

Jen was attempting to look anywhere but at him. Her cheeks were darkened in what he'd like to believe wasn't embarrassment.

Humans have mores against certain types of social nudity the wolves do not. He couldn't remember the details. "Does seeing me unclothed bother you, Jen? Should I endeavor to wear a certain amount of clothing, for your comfort?" It wouldn't be for his own comfort, that was certain. *But I am a guest in her home, and I will bend to her sensibilities while I am.*

Her gaze strayed to his cock. Adrien pretended not to notice, wrapping the gauze while she considered her answer.

Her scent took on a sublime musky edge that broadcast her interest. His cock went hard that quickly, and her eyes widened. Adrien cut the wrap and tied it off.

Jen looked away, her breathing slightly ragged. "No. You need to shift to protect us. I guess...whatever you're accustomed to wearing is fine."

He could do that from wearing jeans, at least, without slowing, but since she was obviously not offended by his nudity, there was no reason to offer that fact. "My thanks. I am most comfortable this way."

Jen focused on the bandage, flexing and tightening her hand.

"Too tight?" he asked, prepared to wrap it again if she said it was.

"No. Just right. Thank you for your help." She pushed to her feet, probably to return to bed.

I want her in my *bed. The pup has no further need of her tonight.* Not that any bed in the cabin was truly his. They were all hers, but his was secluded and...*mine.*

Adrien took the initiative to cup her chin in his fingers and draw her face up, so he could meet her gaze. Jen didn't question him, though her stunning blue eyes asked silent inquiries about his purpose.

"I would do nearly anything you asked," he vowed.

"Anything?"

Adrien dipped his head and parted her lips in a leisurely kiss. Jen didn't balk at it, and he deepened it, making his intentions clear. Her passion unleashed was appealing to him, man and wolf, and he growled in need held momentarily in check.

Jen pulled away abruptly.

Adrien caught her by the shoulders before she could bolt. "It is not a sound of warning," he assured her. "I would never hurt you."

Something that looked suspiciously like panic flashed in her expression. She buried it deep and fast, making him wonder how ingrained hiding it was for her. "We shouldn't do this."

His brow tightened in confusion. He knew she wanted to. What was stopping her? "Jen—?"

"We shouldn't." She shook off his hold and ran for the bedroom she shared with the Keif. At the door, she looked back at him, seemingly saddened. "Thank you again for the bandage."

Then she disappeared from view, and the door closed behind her. Adrien stood there, confused and aching for sex with her. Her scent echoed in his lungs.

That confused him further. How could so sensual a woman, clearly interested in him, deny herself that way? Why would she?

It must be a human thing I don't understand. No female wolf would act so out of character.

Chapter Seven

Jen sat on the porch swing, a thick, oversized sweater pulled tight around her. By comparison, both Adrien and Keif stood in the high grass, naked and apparently comfortable in the chill night air.

"Drink in the moon's essence, my Keif."

"A wolf doesn't need the moon to shift," his pupil countered.

"Once he learns to shift and becomes strong, no. Until then, the moon's power will help fuel the shift."

Keif nodded solemnly, then spread his arms and tipped his head back. Adrien paced around him, every muscle rippling in a way that made Jen's heart palpitate.

"Picture the wolf. Feel the beat of his heart. Hear what he hears. Smell the richness of the soil and the heavy scent of green, growing things."

Jen leaned toward them, holding her breath at the sight of Keif's hair standing on end. His arms and legs thinned and lengthened, his hands thickened and shrank into paws, and red-brown fur sprouted and spread up his back and arms. Highlights of red-gold glimmered in the night lights.

He wobbled, and Adrien lunged toward him, reaching out to steady him. "Let yourself fold into—"

The change came so quickly, Jen couldn't track it. In the blink of an eye, Keif was on all fours, snapping at Adrien, growling, his lips drawn back to bare his teeth, fully a wolf though much smaller than Adrien's wolf was. The lighter fur on his scalp bristled in warning.

Adrien jumped back out of his reach, shifting as quickly as the Keif had. For a moment, they stared at each other. Then the giant wolf that was Adrien bounded away into the trees.

Keif plopped to his backside in the grass, his tongue lolling out and his head cocked, as if something confused him. A moment later, he tore off in the direction Adrien had taken.

Jen sat there, stunned by the speed of events. Adrien had postulated it would take weeks to teach Keif to shift properly and fully.

Maybe his father...sire had been teaching him before he died. Or his dam. It was yet another reminder that she couldn't raise Keif.

Jen pushed it away, searching for signs of their return. From far away, she heard one wolf yip and a second answer. She winced. Hopefully, no one was around to report wild dogs or wolves to the rangers.

The night turned cold, and Jen considered going in. *No. I want to wait until Keif comes home. Back,* she corrected herself. This wasn't his home. It couldn't be his home. Not for long, anyway.

They appeared, streaking from the trees as if racing back to the cabin. Adrien slowed, seemingly letting Keif win. The pup leapt up on the cabin porch and stood before her, legs trembling, chest heaving, thick drool dripping from his tongue.

"Is he okay?" she asked, not sure whether to expect a response or not.

"He's just tired. The Keif has not regained all of his strength yet."

Jen peeked at Adrien, admiring his sweat-soaked skin. Keif jumped up on the swing next to her and laid down, placing his head in her lap with a sigh.

She stared at him, alarm bells going off in her mind. "Shouldn't you teach him to shift back? Before he works himself to exhaustion, I mean."

He passed her by, offering Jen a tantalizing view of his backside. "The shift tires us. Being in wolf form or human form doesn't, in and of itself." He stopped and looked down at Keif. "He is too young to keep his wolf shape while he sleeps, though. His unconscious mind still thinks of his shape as human. When he starts to dream, the Keif will shift to his human shape automatically."

"But shouldn't he learn to shift willingly in both directions?"

"He will in time. For now, he needs to know how to shift to wolf form, for his own protection. He's faster in this form, more agile, has better senses, and he's armed. Teaching him to shift back to human form can take as much time as it needs to."

Jen combed her fingers through Keif's fur, noting that his breathing was slowing. She looked up to thank Adrien, but he was gone.

Keif changed position. One paw fluttered in movement. A low whine escaped his mouth. A boy appeared in the place of the animal, his legs and arms flexing and bunching in his sleep.

She moved her hands this way and that, trying to decide how to lift him without waking him.

"Let me," Adrien whispered.

Jen looked up at him, her heart sinking at the sight of him dressed in jeans. *Stop it. What good will drooling over him do you?*

He lifted Keif and started to turn toward the door. Adrien stopped, and his gaze met hers. There was something potent in that look, something that said her night wasn't as close to over as she'd believed.

****

Jen peeked in at Keif, smiling at the sight of him asleep on the chair with his mother's pillow and his blanket.

The heat at her back sent her heart into overdrive, and Jen pushed the door closed and turned to face him. Adrien's expression left no doubt what he wanted.

This is a really bad idea. But Jen couldn't deny she wanted him. She'd spent half the night reliving the kiss they'd shared the night before. She'd never been kissed that fully before, and she wanted more.

There was no reason to refuse him. He was a wolf on the prowl. Literally. There would be no lies between them, no false promises. Chances were, they couldn't even reproduce together.

She reached a hand out and placed it on his bare chest, reveling in the heat pouring off of his body.

He nodded and eased his face down to hers, capturing her lips in a kiss. She took a step back, coming up against the wall; Adrien followed, his large body crowding hers.

Jen moaned into Adrien's mouth, her body in overdrive. His taste and scent were intoxicating, and her head spun pleasantly.

Adrien lifted her and started moving. It wasn't until a door squeaked that she pulled away and looked around.

Her face blazed in understanding. Adrien was taking her to her father's room. Of course, it was the only open bedroom in the cabin.

"I'll fix the squeak tomorrow," he promised.

"What about Keif?"

A dangerous smile pulled up at his lips. "Pups sleep heavily, especially while they heal and while they are learning to shift. Both cost them a lot of energy."

Part of Jen argued the damage they could do to Keif if he woke to the sounds of them having sex. The rational half admitted Adrien was right. Once Keif was asleep, he rarely moved for the next ten hours, and waking him before he was ready to wake was nearly impossible.

"Jen?"

On my father's bed?

Jen gazed into Adrien's golden eyes, and flutters of anticipation lit in her belly. *Oh yes.*

As if she'd answered aloud, Adrien started walking. He swung the bedroom door shut behind them. At the side of the bed, he paused. Just when Jen would have questioned him, Adrien started talking.

"I can use a condom if you want, but you aren't fertile at the moment."

It was the absolute last discussion she wanted to have with Adrien. *Especially now.* Jen brought her lips to his again, pulling at him to speed him along to something she was sure would be much more enjoyable.

He laid her on the bed and followed her down, his cock nestled at the apex of her thighs.

Where I want him to be. Now.

Adrien pulled back, then pushed to kneeling, astride her legs. He pulled the sweater off the ends of her hands and tossed it on top of the bureau against the far wall.

She licked her lips, savoring the feel of his kiss echoing in her mouth.

"Enjoy?" he teased.

"You kiss so different." Even now, Jen was trying to quantify everything that set him aside from human men.

Adrien looked down at her, bemused. "Different? How do I kiss differently than human men do?"

"More...intense. And your tongue is a little rough. Like a kitten's tongue."

"All the better to eat you with, my dear."

Jen didn't ask how many times he'd used that line. She nodded eagerly, hoping it was an offer.

There was no long, slow strip. Adrien removed her clothes in efficient movements, then his own.

"You don't waste time," she noted. Jen surveyed his body breathlessly, hungry for all of this hard-bodied man.

"A buck takes what he wants. Especially a buck with the skills and drive to someday be an alpha."

"What about what the woman wants?"

He smiled. "If a female didn't want me, she would have made that clear long ago."

"How?"

"She-wolves have claws and very sharp teeth. If one isn't receptive to the idea, there will be no question about it." Adrien paused for a moment and met her eyes. "Are you, Jen?"

"Am I..." What was he asking?

One rough finger stroked at her clit, bringing her off the mattress. "So receptive," he breathed.

Before she could form the words to agree, Adrien had her legs spread wide and was feasting on her, his rough tongue scraping pleasantly at her inner walls.

No wonder women like textured condoms and sex toys.

Jen squirmed beneath him, the wealth of sensation flooding her mind. She'd never felt anything like this before. He was playing at her nerve endings like a master musician at a Stradivarius.

Sounds she tried to stifle broke free. As if that shattered his self-control, Adrien's eating went from attentive to ravenous. Catching her breath was abruptly difficult, and climax crashed over her like a tsunami.

It's been too long. She hadn't let any man touch her sexually since Tyler. Until Adrien, she'd never thought she would again.

Adrien laid a kiss on her still-spasming center and withdrew. He lay down beside her and rolled to his back, stroking patterns on her lower abdomen with his fingertips.

When she recovered enough to question him, Jen turned to look at him directly.

"Are you ready to continue?" he asked, abruptly serious.

Words deserted her for a moment.

"Jen?"

"Did you just suggest that I'm not up to having sex with you?"

"No! I would never—"

She moved down the bed, and silence fell between them. Jen engulfed his cock in her mouth, determined to prove to him she was more than a match for him.

Adrien sucked in a breath, as she started moving. At the second withdrawal and return down his length, he growled, a fierce, animal sound that made her heart trip in excitement. His hips started stroking up and down, allowing her to concentrate on taunting him with her tongue, while he kept the depth at an even level.

"Fucking good," he breathed. "I never realized."

Realization came in a flash. This wasn't something wolves typically did.

I'm taking his cherry. At least part of it.

Jen doubled her efforts, and his hips started moving in jerking motions instead of shifting smoothly. His breathing degraded into gasps and growls. His hands opened and closed, moving aimlessly over the sheet, as if he was afraid he might accidentally harm her if he touched her.

"Stop!"

She ignored him, certain that it was the novelty of coming this way unnerving him.

Adrien's hands closed on her upper arms, and he yanked her off of him. Her fear melted into confusion at the sight of his wide-eyed stare.

He pulled her hand to his cock and closed it around the head, moaning. Before Jen could make sense of it, his cum started to fountain, splashing against her abdomen and her pubic curls. His girth increased by a full twenty-five percent, and she gaped at it, stunned.

This is what he was afraid of. I didn't know he was going to engorge this way. If he had been in my mouth when he did it, I might have choked. Or bitten him.

Adrien's breathing eased, and he stroked a hand through her hair. She smiled at that. Now it was time to see how he handled climax.

****

His mind was still humming in sensual awareness when Jen licked at the head of his cock. He jerked in surprise, and she closed her mouth around him again. In moments, she was moving up and down his length.

Adrien fought for breath, his mind scattered by the alien sensation. In wolf sex, the male was usually the aggressor, but the female held sway over whether or not the male got what he wanted, in the end. Always. Knowing she had final call, she-wolves were selfish lovers, and the males were giving. It wasn't uncommon for a male to pleasure a female and still be denied access to her. He'd never encountered a female who concerned herself with his pleasure this way.

At the same time, the wolf in him protested her being the aggressor. Wolves were equals in most things, and males were never completely subservient. The challenge fired his need to take control, and his teeth extended in show.

In the next heartbeat, he moved. Jen was over him, then beneath him before she could catch her breath. She stared up at him, her fear dissipating. She looked at his fangs in seeming fascination.

Before he could state his intentions, she raised her head and sealed her mouth to his in a kiss. Her tongue dueled with his. She trailed it over his teeth, and a moan escaped her throat.

Adrien pulled back, reminding himself that he was an alpha buck. Lioness or not, he was going to give to Jen until he exhausted them both.

All of her is mine. Every delicious millimeter of her body.

That thought firmly in mind, he started to explore, nipping at her skin as he went. Jen arched and turned, offering herself to him for it. A mad need to mark her as his own ripped a growl from him.

Adrien shook it off and moved on. Her breasts drew his attention, and he suckled at them. Jen shouted, trembling in what he was certain was pleasure.

The meat of her belly was soft and inviting, not packed muscle as most young she-wolves had. He suddenly understood why so many male wolves indulged with human females. Everything about them was soft and inviting, the pleasure without the pain.

He reached Jen's slit again. Her unique flavor and the heat radiating off of her went straight to his head, and Adrien moaned. She was sweet with just a hint of musk.

He'd eaten at females before, usually to appease a young she-wolf who wasn't certain he would measure up to her standards for a sexual partner. Though he wanted to please Jen, this wasn't about gaining her permission. Every sound and movement said he had that already.

On the contrary, he wanted her lost in sexual bliss before he felt the grip of her inner muscles around his cock. He wanted to savor a female who wouldn't leave scars on his back in demand.

As if Jen was voicing her approval of his plan, a litany of 'oh yes' escaped her lips. She moaned, bit at her lower lip, then shuddered, coming hard against his mouth.

Adrien spread her legs wider, feasting on her cream. Shouts and pleas filled the air. Jen came unhinged around him, moving restlessly. She bowed up from the mattress and climaxed for him again.

That pushed Adrien to the limits of his endurance. He moved, bringing his weeping cock to her slit. Though he hadn't asked for her permission, she invited him with another string of 'oh yes'.

Her inner muscles bit hard against him, a sweet pleasure-pain. Either it had been a long time for Jen, or her previous partner had been a very small man.

'Oh yes' became 'Adrien, please', and he started thrusting in earnest. Jen shifted against him, forcing him to the hilt inside her.

"I want to feel it," she whispered.

That confused him. "You don't feel me now?"

"Yes. Oh yes." She thrust her hips up again.

His move to question that ended on her next statement.

"I want to feel you come inside me. I want to feel you... Oh!" She moaned. "I want to feel you grow."

Hearing her say it was a dozen times the aphrodisiac a she-wolf's claws were. "You will," he vowed. *More than once, I promise.*

Adrien let himself go, giving to her as he would a willing she-wolf. Jen grasped at his hips, and he tensed, anticipating the bite of claws. The tender scratches of her human nails were a delight to his senses.

The sensation pushed him to the edges of climax, and he didn't fight it as he would with a she-wolf. Adrien lodged himself tight in her, his cock erupting into her heat. Her inner muscles clenched down rhythmically, and he engorged into her welcoming body.

Jen panted, her body taut. Adrien took it as a challenge. He pressed her into the mattress, growling in reminder that she was his to play at, though she couldn't understand the wolf language.

She wrapped her hands around his face and brought her mouth to his. Something in that move soothed his wolf. The kiss went on and on, lending a potent edge to the feeling of his cock wedged tight in her body.

The kiss didn't end when he lessened within her. Neither did he leave her body. One sexual encounter led to another...then a third. By the time Jen retreated to the room she shared with the Keif, Adrien suspected he might never have enough of this particular female.

Chapter Eight

Three days later

Adrien smiled at the sound of Jen moving around the room with him. Though it was far earlier than he would typically wake, spending time with her had quickly become a valued part of his existence. The time he spent away from her, investigating the dens related to the Keif, was a torture for him, and her nightly forays into his bed were a joy.

The night before was the first time she hadn't retreated to the room she shared with the Keif after they'd burned off their passion, and waking with her still in the bed with him was an unexpected pleasure.

The sound of her leaving the room made his heart stutter. Adrien rushed to leave the bed and pulled his jeans on. He followed her to the kitchen, unsurprised that she was busy making coffee. Jen was as fond of it as he was himself.

She'd pulled one of his collared shirts on over her underwear, and the sight of her in his clothing brought up an alien possessive streak up in him. His cock came to life, demanding another taste of her before the pup started to stir.

Adrien crossed the room and turned her into his arms, bringing his mouth down on hers in a fierce hunger. Jen didn't shy from the move. Her body scented, and her tongue dueled with his. A moan of want escaped her busy mouth and invaded his.

The sound of movement caught his attention. It wasn't the pup. It came from outside, and it was a large body moving. Most likely male. But not stealthy enough to be a wolf. What human had business here? This was Jen's home.

As if she felt the change in his kiss—and she might have, Jen pulled away slightly and whispered his name. Adrien brought his lips to within millimeters of hers, but he moved slightly to avoid her attempt to kiss him again. She opened her eyes, seemingly hurt by his refusal.

Before she could question him, he formed one of his own and breathed it against her cheek. "Are you expecting someone?"

She shook her head. "No. I would have told you if I was."

He'd suspected that. "Go to your room. Lock yourself in with the Keif. Dress, in case we have to run."

Jen eased out of his arms and hurried to comply. Adrien didn't relax until he heard the door lock.

No time to let my guard down. He headed for the outside door, intent on tracking and finding his prey. No one would impose upon Jen without her express invitation while he was there to prevent it. No one would endanger her, wolf or not.

Adrien yanked the door open...and came face-to-face with Cal. It took a moment to reason his muscles loose. This man was an ally. Jen trusted him, and she had good instincts.

"Come in, Cal," he invited, certain that Jen would do the same. "What brings you here?"

He hesitated for a moment before he stepped inside, shifting a large box in his hands to accomplish the task. Cal's musk said he was furious. Was something wrong? Had he seen the kiss and had something to say about it?

Fuck him, if he thinks he can order me away from Jen. Mother Moon help him, if he thinks he can order Jen away from the Keif and from me.

"I brought supplies. I wasn't sure how much chance you've had to stock up." He set the box on the table.

"Thank you, but I took care of that." Was Cal insinuating Adrien was incapable of providing for those under his protection? Probably not. Chances were, he was concerned for Jen. *She doesn't need him to be.*

"I brought some of Jen's favorites."

Adrien nodded. "Then I do thank you for that." But it also irked him that another male knew her favorites, when Adrien could only guess.

I can use this as a learning experience. I will note everything Cal brought with him.

Jen let herself out of the bedroom, still dressed in Adrien's shirt, but with a pair of jeans beneath it now. He smiled her direction. If Cal had any intentions toward Jen, the way she was dressed would surely dissuade the human.

"Good morning, Cal," she called out. "Would you like some coffee?"

"I would love some."

She went to the steaming pot, then pulled down three large mugs from the cabinet. Both men made their way to her and took their mugs in turn. Adrien let Cal take his first, not because he was deferring to him, but because Jen had offered to make him a cup. She would find it rude if he intercepted that mug.

Adrien sipped his black, as did Cal. Jen went to the fridge and poured half-n-half in hers.

Cal reached into the box and pulled out a smaller, white box that smelled of sugar. He set it on the table, popped open the tape holding it shut, then waved Jen toward it.

She pulled out a confection covered in powdered sugar and with a short stack of white frosting piled on one side. A moan of delight rumbled from her as she bit into the treat.

It took Adrien a moment to identify it as a doughnut. It wasn't something he typically ate, so it had never been important to know what it was before. *It is now. If Jen likes them, she will have them.*

Cal smiled. "You were always a sucker for those." He sipped his coffee again.

"Why do you think I avoid going to *Heavenly.* If I stopped there for coffee every day, I would weigh three hundred pounds."

Adrien doubted she was being serious. At the same time, he committed two things to memory:

the name of the place she preferred to get her doughnuts and the fact that this was an occasional treat and not a daily one.

"I also talked to Sandra."

Adrien waited to hear what came next, unsure of who Sandra was or why Jen would care about her.

She swallowed a mouthful of the cake, powder dusting her chin. Adrien ached to lick it off for her, but that wasn't something he intended to do in front of Cal.

Jen nodded. "And?"

"She's considering you officially on leave. She's using some of that back stock of vacation time you have on the books and calling this a family emergency."

"Good. That means I have at least a month. Did she give the files to Howard I asked her to?"

"Yes."

Adrien drank a mouthful of his coffee, committing more facts to memory. *Jen rarely takes the breaks her job affords her. Her boss's name is Sandra. She trusts a coworker named Howard more than the others.* Listening to her speak to Cal was a good way to learn more about Jen.

Cal finished his coffee and placed the mug in the sink. "Well, I have to get going. Meetings at ten and noon."

Jen paused in sucking the sugar off her fingertip. "Thanks so much for taking care of that, Cal."

He nodded, then turned toward the door. Cal paused and glanced Adrien's direction. "Got a minute?"

Adrien ground his teeth on a half a dozen challenges, then offered a snap of his head in agreement. Though it was clear the detective and Jen were nothing more than friends, Adrien sensed that Cal saw himself as more.

No one warns off an alpha buck. The sooner Cal learned that, the less chance the human would end up regretting his words.

Cal led him out of the cabin and toward the path back to the road. The grass caressed the soles of Adrien's feet, and he calmed himself. There was no sense going into this with the thought of teaching Cal a physical lesson.

The detective stopped and turned to glare at Adrien.

Unless he wants to start a fight, he amended.

Cal didn't hesitate. "If you hurt her in any way—physically or emotionally—I will form a hunting party, wolf."

Not what I expected. Adrien had expected Cal to warn him off. Uncertainty about what Cal thought his place in Jen's life was assaulted Adrien for the first time. This wasn't a male with interest in her. It was a male acting the part of a sire.

"Do we understand each other?" The challenge was impossible to miss.

"I would never purposefully hurt Jen, and if I—"

"Take care that you don't. Not accidentally. Not purposefully. Kid gloves, buddy."

A whisper of sound over his right shoulder him warned Adrien of Jen's approach. The shifting wind brought her scent to confirm it.

I'm running out of time to find out what his aim is. "I am always careful with women. Why don't you tell me why Jen requires *extreme* care?"

Cal snapped his head around, and his cheeks darkened. "She does," he breathed so low Jen might miss it but Adrien wouldn't.

"You are kidding me," Jen complained. "Cal, tell me you're not trying to manage my affairs, now."

The detective winced. "Of course not."

"Then what is going on here?" Jen stopped a step ahead of Adrien and to his right, then turned to bring both males into her field of vision, though in profile. She focused on Adrien and raised an eyebrow, indicating she wanted him to answer her.

Gently. "Cal warned me to be nice. Big bad wolf and all that." He shrugged, trying to make light of it.

Jen shot a look of exasperation at Cal.

Before she could lodge a protest, Cal defended himself. "I worry. This isn't a usual occurrence for you, Jen."

Adrien felt the fur at the back of his head bristle. *Fucking a wolf?* The idea of her with any of his pack mates made Adrien's teeth ache for a good ass kicking. *It's a damned good thing she doesn't sleep with wolves often.* Adrien was quickly becoming territorial.

Jen interrupted his internal argument. "I'm a big girl, Cal. I can date who I want to date."

Date? Adrien liked the sound of that. Wolves didn't date. They fucked or mated. Occasionally, they teased or flirted.

"But you haven't since..." Cal paled a notch.

Jen looked close to tears at the mention of whatever hadn't been said. Before Adrien could gather her into his arms, she composed herself and cleared her throat.

"I will date who I choose to." That stated firmly, she turned on her heel and walked away.

Cal's expression said he wanted to crawl into a deep hole and pull the soil in after him. He watched her walk away, looking forlorn.

Adrien took his time. "Your interest in her isn't sexual," he prompted.

"No. Jen has always been sort of a little sister to me."

"What happened to her that you're afraid of a man hurting her?"

Cal didn't reply.

The need to know ate at Adrien. "Was she raped? Abducted? Abus—"

"If Jen trusts you enough to tell you, she will." His tone announced that the subject was closed.

Adrien glanced toward the cabin, but Jen had retreated inside already. "Right. Is there anything you *will* tell me?"

"Kid gloves. Hunting party. Any questions?"

"No. I think that's fairly clear."

Cal offered a grunt that reminded Adrien of his sire. Then he walked away.

Adrien hesitated a moment. He made his way back into the cabin. Jen wasn't in the kitchen or the living room. He went to the bedroom she'd given him, his heart heavy in the certainty that she'd retreated to the one she shared with Michael.

There was little question she'd been sorely used, but Adrien had no clue what the situation was. As such, he didn't know what he should or shouldn't do, and that was the equivalent of finding himself on a muddy slope.

He stopped in the doorway to his room, stunned by the sight of Jen sitting on the bed, nude, mouthwateringly inviting.

If she's willing and not upset with me, the questions of what happened to her in the past can wait.

Adrien shut the door and crossed the room to her, peeling his button fly open on the way.

Chapter Nine

One week later

Adrien watched Jen sleep. It was early for her, not even dinner time yet, but the late nights of Adrien teaching the Keif to shift and the two of them testing their shared passion had finally caught up with her. Hopefully, she would wake for dinner, refreshed. If she didn't, he would be torn between letting her get the rest she needed and seeing to the food her body required.

He placed his hand near enough to her back to feel the heat radiating off her body. If he didn't fear waking her, he would touch, savoring every centimeter of her soft skin.

No. If I do that, it will surely head toward more she's not comfortable doing while the pup is awake. If she were a she-wolf, there would be no such concern, but Jen was not a wolf, and she felt it unwise to expose the Keif to noises of sexuality that was not that of his sire and dam. With Adrien as the Keif's protector—his guardian, it was to be expected that the Keif might be exposed to such things, but it was not acceptable to the human mores she held to.

While it frustrated him to wait to indulge with her, he found it endearing that she worried for the pup so. He could easily picture Jen as a most caring dam to some lucky pups.

My pups!

Adrien pulled his hand back and left the bed, his emotions rioting. He knew what he wanted from her, but it wasn't something wolves did often. Though the wolf genes were dominant and the young not compromised by having a human dam, bias against intermixing the species ran deep.

To his knowledge, an Enforcer had never taken a human mate, though the Enforcer was expected to deal closely with humans.

But I want her, and I won't be *Enforcer, once my sire is no longer Tragen.* That day was still a decade or more off, though. *I don't intend to wait that long to make Jen my mate.*

What would his sire say if Adrien returned to the den with a human mate and half-bred pups? Would he even be welcome? He was sure he wouldn't be if it were up to his brother Viktor.

Viktor isn't Tragen. He will never be *Tragen, unless someone kills the Keif. And if he did turn me away from the den, I have the apartment, and Jen has the cabin. We don't have to live in the den.*

Why am I arguing this?

Because I want her! I want her to be dam to my pups!

He stalked out of the bedroom, frustrated with himself for his indecision. Was mating with Jen a good idea or bad? What if she wasn't willing to mate and only wanted a fuck buddy? What if mating would be detrimental for her?

"Troubled, Enforcer?" the Keif asked.

He winced at the truth that the pup surely knew he was. "Yes."

"You will have what you want, if you allow her time."

Adrien stopped short, staring at the Keif in shock. "What?"

"If you wait, Jen will advance the subject with you. Until she does, she is not ready for you to suggest it."

"What subject?"

Michael looked up from the toys scattered around his feet and glared at him. "You want Jen as your mate. She will be, in time."

He wanted to ask how much time, but it was a safe bet the Keif couldn't tell him that. His visions were surely not that reliable yet. Michael had already admitted he wasn't certain he would see events in a timely fashion.

The Keif tipped his head to one side, his gaze far away. "Your pups together will be fierce and respected. They will grow strong, and they will be sought after as mates." He picked up a toy train and focused his attention on spinning the wheels.

Adrien squatted to his level, his heart hammering in excitement. "You have seen this?"

"Yes."

"But I must wait for Jen to ask me?" It wasn't the usual way among wolves.

"If you wish to succeed."

"I do." Another question begged answer. "Will we ever live at my home den?"

Michael met his gaze, starkly serious. "Does it matter to you?"

With the promise of Jen as my mate? "No."

He nodded and went back to playing.

****

Jen had been in a fitful sleep for an hour, but Adrien was too keyed up to rest. At last, he abandoned the bed and headed for her office.

The furnishings were heavy and dark, indicating that it had been her sire's office before it had been hers. The computer was only a few years old, certainly too new to have belonged to Andrew Verik.

Adrien fired it up and stared at the browser for a long moment. *Why am I questioning this? I know why I came to the computer.*

He suspected he didn't want to know what had happened to Jen. He feared he was shying from finding out. After all, he'd wasted two days without investigating it.

An alpha buck always protects what is his, whether it is a mate, child, or a lover. Disgusted with himself for his indecision, Adrien started a search of the local news site. *Something happening to Andrew Verik's daughter must have been news.*

The entries came up with the newest first. Jen's career in Child Protection was as distinguished as her sire's had been with the police force. The latter had been the Lion. Jen was every ounce her sire's get.

It was four pages before he found what he was looking for. Adrien read article after article, his blood running cold. According to the articles, it had been a chance encounter. A human male had grabbed Jen off the street and beaten her badly. When two of her sire's officers had intervened, both of them had been shot by her attacker before one—*Cal*—had gotten off a lucky shot and killed the criminal. Cal and Jen had survived. The other officer had not.

Pictures of a battered Jen, shell-shocked, leaving the hospital wrapped in her sire's arms, made him wince. She'd nearly lost her life. What would that do to a woman?

Adrien kept reading, hungry for information, but reading sparked more questions than it answered. Something was seriously wrong with the story the articles told. Unless the criminal—Regis—was a wolf, it simply wasn't believable that he could perform the superhuman feats attributed to him.

If he was a wolf, I would know about the attack.

If Regis had the type of skills the articles attributed to him, he wouldn't be beating up women to make a few bucks in a mugging. *He'd be a damned hired gun...and a good one at that.*

If Regis wasn't that good—which went without saying, there had been one hell of a cover-up. *But why?*

It was a safe bet Jen wouldn't cover for Cal doing something illegal. Cal would cover for Jen, but what would Jen be involved in that would require a cover-up? The only thing Adrien could come up with would be if Jen had killed Regis

herself...or accidentally killed the other officer—
Tyler Stabol—in an attempt to kill Regis, and
everyone involved had hidden it to keep her out of
the public eye.

For some reason, he kept coming back to
Stabol. There was something wrong there. For all
that Regis was a street punk made out to look like
he had super powers, Stabol was reported to be a
golden boy officer with a bright future, but he
hadn't even gotten a shot off before he was killed.

There was something off kilter about this
situation, and Cal had the answers to what that
might be. Adrien closed the computer, made his
way outside, and pulled out his cell phone. He
dialed the cell number Cal had given him when he
visited the cabin the last time.

Cal answered on the first ring. "What's
wrong?" he asked urgently.

"Tell me about Stabol."

The hiss on the other side of the phone
announced clearly that Cal wasn't happy about
the question.

Too bad. "I'm waiting."

"What did she tell you?" he side-stepped
answering.

"Nothing," Adrien admitted. "I did my own
research. I know the official story doesn't add up.
You know it doesn't. I want you to tell me my
suspicions aren't true, because at least they make
sense."

Jen is not a killer. That was one fact Adrien
was sure of.

Cal sighed, and sounds of the older man moving confirmed that Adrien had struck a nerve. At last, Cal spoke.

"What do you think happened?"

"I know there's no way Regis shot both you and Stabol before one of you got off a shot and killed him. I *wonder* what ballistics would say about who killed whom?"

He grumbled something that sounded suspiciously like "Good instincts." A second sigh escaped him. "Regis's gun did take Stabol down. Mine took down Regis."

Two down. One to go. "Whose gun really took you down? Stabol's?" It was a shot in the dark and answered nothing.

"Yeah. Stabol's. The bastard."

It was both a surprise and not. "In what order?"

"I shot Regis. I had no choice. He would have shot Jen."

The wolf raised its head at the long-ago threat to its woman. *My mate!* Adrien forced it back. He needed to think...not react. "Considering the shot you took, he was as good as dead before he hit the ground."

"He was." There was a potent pause. "Which means—"

"Regis *didn't* shoot Stabol, but his gun did. Who shot Stabol? You? Did you lose your own weapon when you were shot and used Regis's, because it was handy?" *No. That doesn't make sense. Why would they hide that from the media?*

‖

"You have to understand the position we were in," Cal began. "I was useless to her. Stabol was over the edge. He had every intention of killing me and then Jen."

Adrien's stomach soured. Jen *had* killed Stabol. "Why?"

Cal didn't question what he meant. He didn't answer it directly either. "You really should ask Jen—"

"She's my mate," Adrien snapped back. "Well...she will be if she accepts me. Whatever the situation was, I will protect her from—"

"This is not a good idea. Suggesting a permanent relationship with her might have...echoes."

Adrien's focus narrowed. "They were engaged to be married?"

Cal hesitated, and a soft sound escaped his lips. "Stabol was a slippery character. He enjoyed the perks dating the Chief's daughter gave him."

"And?" Adrien prompted him. "I don't believe Jen just imagined more. She's not the type."

"Oh, Stabol *said* he was going to marry her, but he never intended to."

Outrage burned in his gut. "What happened? What brought it to a head?"

Cal was silent so long Adrien was sure he wasn't going to answer.

"He got Jen pregnant. So, you see... If he married her, he was trapped in a marriage he didn't really want. If he didn't, Andy would have made his life hell for what he was doing to Jen. To

Stabol's mind, playing the part of heartbroken, love-lost victim was preferable to either of those choices."

Bile rose in Adrien's throat. "He hired Regis to..." He couldn't force the words out. *Stabol's lover. The woman who was promised marriage. The woman who was carrying his child.*

"We don't know what Stabol had on Regis...or what he promised him. We do know he wanted Jen beaten and killed."

His hackles rose. "And he wanted to watch her die? What reason did he have for being there?" How cold was the bastard?

"Two reasons. The first was that he wanted to make sure Regis followed through. Actually, left to his own devices, Stabol wouldn't have gotten what he wanted out of Regis."

That surprised him. "What do you mean by that?"

"While she was begging Regis to stop, Jen apparently told him she was pregnant. When I got there, Stabol had a gun to Regis's head, ordering him to finish the job."

An involuntary shudder ripped through Adrien at the thought of Jen hearing her lover order that.

Cal continued, seemingly glad to be able to share the tale with someone after years of silence. "Regis was terrified of killing an unborn child. An innocent. He was more afraid of dying, though.

"Of course, Stabol wouldn't be able to risk letting Regis live. The other reason he was there... His plan would have included delivering Jen's killer to Andy...and making sure Regis couldn't roll over and give Stabol's name to the police the next time he got picked up for a crime."

"That's true enough." Stabol wouldn't have risked Regis outing him for his involvement in Jen's murder.

"Regis's change of heart came too late. The beating itself..."

"She lost her child." Adrien's heart ached for Jen. *No wonder she's a Lioness when she's protecting children.*

But there was still a burning question he had to ask. "What were *you* doing there, Cal?"

"Jen told me. That she was pregnant. That they were leaving to elope that night. Where she was meeting Stabol. I didn't trust the bastard. Never had. There was always something...off about him."

"You followed him...or her," Adrien guessed.

"Him. If I'd followed Jen, things wouldn't have gotten as far as they had. I've been protecting her ever since. The psychologists would probably say it's unhealthy, but I can't get the picture of her out of my mind."

Lying on the pavement. Crying. Begging. Bleeding. "You're not the only one. I intend to protect her, even if she's not capable of accepting me as her mate after Stabol."

Cal took his time answering. "I hope she can. She's better with you. A part of Jen is alive now that I thought had died that night."

"Thanks." It meant a lot to him that Cal trusted him, though he'd never cared what a human thought about him before.

"Call me if you need anything." With that, he was gone.

Adrien closed the phone and stared at the stars for a moment. Then he ambled back into the cabin and eased into bed with Jen.

She turned to him and wrapped her arms around him.

Please, accept me. Ask the question the Keif says is lurking inside you.

Chapter Ten

Two days later

"You shouldn't hesitate, Jen."

She looked up in surprise at Keif's statement. "What?"

He settled beside her, dressed—as Adrien often was—in a pair of jeans and nothing more. Keif had even started brushing his hair to look more like Adrien's. It seemed he was patterning himself more and more after Adrien every day.

"I know you've wondered if you and Adrien could ever be more to each other than what you have now."

"How do you—?"

Keif raised an eyebrow in seeming disbelief.

"Oh. Yes. You have visions of the future." She wished she did. She might not feel so lost that way. "What shouldn't I hesitate about?"

"Ask Adrien to show you how wolves mate."

Her cheeks darkened at the thought of taking sexual advice from a child. *He's not human, and wolf mores on nudity are much different.* She wondered if the young wolves saw older wolves having sex, at least pups seeing their parents. In many human cultures, it was the norm.

Keif continued. "I saw what happened to you with that...human. Stabol."

Jen choked at the memories. *He'd seen that?*

As if answering her, Keif nodded. "When I scratched you. I apologize again, but the vision was so potent, I lost control."

She nodded. "I understand that." She'd lost control at the memories more than a few times in her life. Jen waited to see what Keif had to say about the matter.

"Accept Adrien as your mate when he asks."

"He *intends* to ask?"

"He's considering it. If you ask him to show you how wolves mate, he won't be able to help himself. He wants to."

"But...?" She couldn't phrase the question. Keif was too young to possibly understand her concerns, despite what he said he'd seen.

Proving her wrong, he laid a hand on her arm and sighed. "Adrien can give you young, Jen. He *wants* you to be dam to his pups. The pups will be strong, able, and they will find happiness with the pack. You have my vow on that. You also have my word that no one will take these pups from you. Not like you lost your last."

It was too much to ask for. Could she trust what Keif was saying was true?

He sighed again, then pushed to his feet. "You have a lot to consider, I know. Think about what I said. Adrien wants you as his mate, and it will end so well for you both."

Before she could find the words to thank him or question him, Keif had disappeared into the room they shared together.

Share anytime I'm not in Adrien's bed. That was fast becoming a nightly occurrence.

Should I ask him? She recalled Adrien's explanation of Keif's gifts. *He sees the future as fact.* Did that mean he already knew she would ask Adrien to show her how wolves mated and already knew they would mate?

It was too much to wrap her head around.

****

Adrien settled into bed next to Jen, heartened that she was here with him. He'd worried she might retreat to the other room instead.

Since he'd come back from hunting with the cleaned and eviscerated carcass of a successful kill, Jen had been distracted...nearly withdrawn. Adrien had worried she'd been bothered by the reality of his animal side, displayed so prominently.

When he'd asked her what was wrong, she'd stated she simply had something on her mind. Not knowing what upset her was the most terrifying thing Adrien had dealt with in years.

Jen trailed a hand down his chest, seemingly considering something of great importance.

"What do you want?" Adrien asked. It wasn't offered lightly. He would give her nearly anything she asked for.

She smiled. "You."

Adrien reached for a condom, ready to fulfill that wish until they both dropped from exhaustion. Jen nibbled at his shoulder, hurrying him along. He ripped the condom wrapper open, cursing the need to use one silently.

"I want you to show me how wolves mate."

He went still, his heart pounding in disbelief. "You want to experience a wolf mating?"

She hummed in pleasure, and reached for his cock, stroking him.

Adrien cupped her face up to his, the condom pressed between her cheek and his fingers. "This isn't something you play at with an intent male, Jen."

She nodded.

Adrien brushed a kiss against her lips, and she tried to deepen the kiss. He pulled back slightly.

"If you want to know how wolves mate, you are inviting me to take you as my mate. Do you understand me?"

Jen searched his expression. "Yes."

"You want to be my mate?" *Say 'yes'. You won't regret it.*

"Yes. I do."

His cock ached to be inside her. "Now?"

She nodded, her lips making soft trails over his chin.

Adrien tossed the condom away. If he was making Jen his mate, damned if he was going to pass on the chance to plant his young while he was doing it.

Especially after what the Keif told him. *Our young will be fierce and respected. As if I had any doubt of that? The Tragen's Enforcer mating with the Lion's daughter? Our young will be the stuff of legends.*

He captured Jen's mouth, pressing her into the pillow. Adrien pulled back, smiling at her ragged breathing.

Her belly quivered under his touch, but he didn't doubt it wasn't in fear. "You will be my mate, Jen."

She nodded.

Adrien spread her nether lips with two fingers and played a finger inside her, holding her down when she shifted to move. "I will protect you always. I will love you as often as you are receptive to me."

Jen moaned, her eyes half-closed in pleasure.

"I am a jealous wolf, when it comes to you. You will be wholly mine, and no male will cross you or touch you without answering to me. You are mine to touch."

"Yes." It was an invitation, if he'd ever heard one.

"Mine to taste." Adrien pulled his hand back and moved to replace it with his mouth.

Jen's flavor was a heady mix of arousal and fertile female that went to his head. She arched beneath him, crying out wildly. She tunneled her fingers in his fur and closed them down tight, tugging him toward the head of the bed.

He refused her order. Adrien was a male in pursuit of his mate, and Jen would have him at his most potent.

The change in her flavor announcing her coming climax made his breathing hitch in excitement. It was nearly time. In moments, she was jerking against his mouth, fractured shouts calling to the predator in him.

My mate. It is time.

Adrien levered himself over her and thrust inside. Jen screamed. She released his fur, and her short nails raked down his chest, prompting a growl from him. Her display wasn't a refusal of him, he knew, and his growl wasn't a warning. In truth, the scratches down his chest spurred him on.

He pounded hard at her body, driven to master her climax, to prove himself worthy of claiming her as his mate. Jen came to climax again, and Adrien came in her wake, reveling in her sheath massaging at his length.

He paused long enough to plunder her mouth, counting the heartbeats his cock remained engorged inside her, desperate to continue his wooing. At last, it subsided, and he went back to work on her.

"Adrien?" she questioned. It seemed she couldn't decide how to phrase the query more specifically.

"Have you decided I am a worthy mate?" he prompted her.

"I already told you I wanted—"

"No, Jen. I cannot finalize the mating, until you ask me to. Until then, I must prove myself to you. Prove I am worthy to proclaim you as my mate and to sire your young." It might already be too late for the latter. He'd spilled inside her in her fertile cycle. His cock leaked more fluids at the thought of her bearing his pup.

"You think I'm not sure?" There was a note of hurt in her tone.

"Then tell me what you want from me and end my torment." Mother Moon, but he lived to hear her say the words.

"This is how a wolf mating is carried out?"

"Yes." *Damn it all.* Adrien had never realized how frustrating it would be.

A sly smile curved her lips.

He cursed fluently at that. Females were all alike, after all. Knowing she had this power over him, Jen intended to prove it. The alpha buck in him wanted to walk away from this insanity. The possessive voice reminded him that, until Jen was bound to him, another male could still claim her.

Never. She is mine. He doubled his efforts, driving Jen over in moments.

"If you don't finish this, I will finish you," she warned. As if to prove it, Jen laid her nails down his chest again, this time drawing a few drops of blood.

Adrien captured her hands and pinned them to the pillow beside her head, keeping watch to make sure she didn't try to bite him. This was almost sinfully easy. A she-wolf would have fought his attempt to immobilize her this way.

I don't want *a she-wolf. I want Jen. The young Lioness. My mate.*

"Adrien," she pleaded. "I told you I want you to finish."

"Then say the words I need to hear."

Her expression went panicked, and he feared her time with Stabol had left her unable to say such a thing to him. Had she learned to fear believing a male worthy of her.

Her face eased a bit. "You're worthy to be my mate," she breathed. Her tone was hopeful, as if she wasn't sure that was what he was waiting for. "I'm convinced of that."

Adrien forced his need to come back brutally. Now that he had her word, he wasn't going to climax until he was ready to lay his mark.

He left her body in a rush and turned her to her stomach. Adrien lifted her at the waist. Then he was back inside her. thrusting downward into her upturned core.

Her sounds rose, encouraging him to stake his claim on her. His fangs descended, and his senses sharpened. Adrien emptied into her body in a rush, and the wildness rose within. He pulled her upright, over his engorging cock, sinking his teeth into her shoulder.

Jen's body clenched down tight on his cock, gripping him nearly painfully tight. She whimpered, driving the hunter in him crazy for more of her.

He suckled at the bite, savoring her blood on his tongue, mindful not to bite down too deeply into the meat of her shoulder. Jen wasn't a wolf.

He had to be gentle with her while he made her his own.

She went still. Then she did what he'd hoped she would. Jen fought him as a she-wolf might in the heat of mating. She raked at his restraining arm, drawing blood. Jen trembled in his arms, gasping for breath.

Adrien released her shoulder, drunk on his mate's blood. "Drink my blood, Jen. Just a little."

She didn't seem to hear him. Just when he was about to repeat himself, Jen stopped clawing at him. Her head dipped slowly, and her mouth closed around the cuts on his forearm. She suckled weakly at him, and Adrien growled, needing more of her.

Her teeth scraped at his arm...then sank in slightly. Adrien reveled in it, lost in bliss. Jen was leaving her mark on him, claiming him as he had claimed her. She would be a jealous Lioness and Mother Moon help any female who thought to get between them.

His cock subsided, and he eased out of her body. He turned Jen toward him, pinned her arms to the headboard of the bed, and thrust inside her again. She focused on his fangs, her eyes widening a notch.

"I will never hurt you," Adrien vowed.

She nodded, then licked his blood from her upper lip. That was too enticing for Adrien to pass up. He parted her lips in a kiss. Jen trailed her tongue over his fangs, vented a moan into his mouth, then came at him in a fervor.

Oh, yes. She is my mate, and nothing can separate us now. The Keif gave his word on that.

****

Jen woke on her stomach in her father's old bed. *Our bed now.* She was tangled in the sheets, and her hair was in complete disarray around her face.

Everything after she told Adrien he was worthy was something of a blur. She vaguely remembered him biting at her shoulder, but strangely it didn't hurt much. Though she knew he'd laid his fangs into her, she would swear there was nothing more than deep scratches on her shoulder. Jen reached back, wincing at the rough scab that had formed overnight.

Voices in the kitchen let her know she'd slept later than Keif had. That was a first in her experience. The voices moved closer, and Jen scrambled to sitting. She pulled the quilt over her, then tucked it beneath her arms.

The door opened, and Keif stepped back to let Adrien enter with a tray of food. Her mouth watered at the sight and scent of a hearty breakfast. After half the night spent in sexual abandon with Adrien, it was no wonder she was hungry.

He set the tray astride her legs and brushed a kiss against her lips. Then he settled on the mattress next to her.

Jen motioned to the food, too stunned to speak for a moment. "This is very sweet. You didn't have to do this."

Keif laughed, and Adrien raised an eyebrow at her that challenged the statement. The younger loped out of the room, off to pursue whatever play he had planned for the morning.

"I don't understand." Surely, she was missing something.

"You asked to know how a wolf mates," he reminded her patiently.

"Yes." But what did that have to do with him delivering her breakfast in bed?

He trailed one rough finger down her nose, then her lips, stopping at the tip of her chin. "You are my mate. I see to your needs. Always. While I am physically with you, I will provide whatever you require of me. For the moment, you need to eat. It is my happy duty to supply it. Of course, I will get you doughnuts from *Heavenly*, if that is what you prefer."

He's only seen me have them once, only heard me mention the place I buy them once, and he remembers it. Had any man ever proven himself that attentive to her needs? Not even her father. "That's something I treat myself to a few times a month."

"Then you are nearly due for it. I will remember that."

She didn't doubt he would. Jen reached toward him and kissed him. The tray rattled, and Adrien steadied it while he indulged.

He pulled away, his eyes hot in promise. "Eat, before your food gets cold."

Jen nodded, and picked up her fork. The tray contained what looked like a lumberjack's breakfast to her: coffee, juice, eggs, country fried potatoes, toast, and even a thick steak. There was no way she could eat all this.

"Is there a problem?" Adrien asked urgently.

"No." It was intended for both of them, of course. The fact that there was only one set of silverware was rather romantic, when she thought about it.

Jen took a bite of the eggs, then filled the fork and offered it to Adrien.

He shook his head, smiling widely. "The Keif and I have already eaten."

She looked at the plate of food again. "Adrien, humans don't eat this much. I admit I built up an appetite last night, but there's no way—"

His laugh stopped her short. "Soon, you will. It is better for me to be prepared for that moment than to fall short when the hunger strikes. And the pup may eat your leavings until then. He is healed, but he is still a growing pup."

His meaning was impossible to miss. The condom he'd opened and then disposed of hadn't escaped her attention. "You think I will? So soon?"

"Yes, I do. And I know the typical gestation of a wolf pup is only five months. When you catch, the need to feed the growing young one will be a pressing concern." He hesitated, seemingly waiting for more questions. "Do you understand, Jen?"

She nodded, then took a bite of the toast before he could order her to eat again.

Adrien watched her eat, smiling faintly. After a few minutes, he shifted on the bed. He ran his fingertips over the lines of scab gently, then leaned down to kiss at it.

Her heart skipped in excitement, and her body awoke to his proximity. *My mate.*

Adrien kissed, again and again, working his way around the mark, then along the upper line of her shoulder to her neck. She tipped her head to the opposite side, giving him room to shower affection on her.

The door closed, and sounds of running feet followed. In the next room, the mattress springs squeaked. Then the radio started up.

Jen smiled at that. Clearly Keif was suggesting they should follow through.

His fang tips scraped lightly at her throat, and she shivered in delight. Adrien was a predator, but he was her mate. He would never hurt her.

"Do you want to eat more?" he asked.

She shook her head. It wasn't a lie. Her stomach was squirming in anticipation.

"Good. I will make you more later." He took the mostly-full tray to the bureau and left it there. In the next moment, he was in bed with her, drawing the quilts from her body.

Jen pulled at his jeans, popping the buttons. She dismissed a momentary qualm about doing this with Keif awake in the next room. They were a mated couple...married, for all intents and purposes. Even if she was a married woman with a foster child, it wouldn't be unexpected that she and her husband would have sex.

That clarified in her mind, she yanked down at Adrien's jeans and pulled him over her.

Chapter Eleven

A week and a half later

Jen paced the kitchen, glancing out the window for signs of Adrien returning in the car. She couldn't name what had her on edge, though she suspected Keif's subdued mood had her nervous that something was coming.

He said he'd warn Adrien if he saw what was coming in time. That indicated he might not see it. She reached for her cell phone, intent on calling Adrien back to the cabin.

A flash of movement in the tree line sent her heart skittering. She snatched up the phone and hit the autodial she'd set to Adrien's number.

It failed almost immediately. There were no bars. *That never happens up here. The booster makes sure I have good reception.* The certainty that they'd used a cell block sent her into motion.

She raced to the bedroom where Keif was taking a nap...and stopped short in the doorway. He wasn't in the bed or on the chair. Jen might have believed he went to the bathroom, but the pillow, blanket, and jacket were all gone as well.

He ran? Without warning me, he ran?

Jen reminded herself that Keif was likely in a panic. If these were the same wolves who'd killed his parents and tried to kill him, he might be too frightened to think clearly. *And too young. He's five. There's a reason children have parents and advocates.*

"Keif, if you can hear me, stay hidden." She prayed he wasn't in the cabin to hear her. If he was, they would surely be able to sniff him out.

Whether he was or not, she had to protect herself. Jen went to her father's den and pulled out the shotgun. Considering the enemies he'd made, he'd gone heavy on the firepower. She chose a gas-powered semiautomatic 12-gauge with a high capacity magazine. Jen had learned to shoot it when she was a teenager. She made her checks, loaded it, and switched off the safety.

She chose her position well. At the end of the hallway, there were no close windows and a narrow route for them to come at her. With a shotgun loaded with buck shot, that was the best she could ask for.

There was no attempt at sneaking up on her. The sound of splintering wood from the kitchen announced a full frontal assault.

Jen raised the barrel, considered that, and lowered it again. Chances were, they were coming in shifted into wolves.

That proved to be true. A dark wolf nearly the size of Adrien's rounded the corner, and she squeezed off the first shot. It dodged right, yelped and faltered—probably due to a pellet or two slamming home—then started moving again. The second shot performed no better.

Before she had a chance to unload a third, the wolf was in human form, one hand locked around her throat and the other pushing the shotgun up and away from his body. The motion forced her finger against the trigger and sent the third shot into the ceiling over her head. Splinters of wood rained down around her. In the next heartbeat, her hand was empty. The shotgun clattered down the hall behind him.

They stared at each other, Jen's breathing ragged. He didn't seem concerned with the blood coursing down his chest and arm.

Of course. He's a wolf. If Keif could regrow bones in a few days, he can heal from a few pellets salting his hide in hours.

But the blood would give Adrien something to track. *Why isn't he concerned about that?*

"Where is the pup?" he demanded.

"I don't know."

His hand tightened for a moment and then loosened again. "Where?"

"He ran. He saw you coming and ran before I had a chance to try and hide him."

"Check it."

The other four wolves were—*thankfully*—dressed in jeans, though unclothed otherwise. They spread out, taking a room apiece. Thumps, rips, and crashes let Jen know she would be doing a lot of redecorating and repairs.

If I survive this. That wasn't looking very likely.

The one holding Jen sniffed the air. His eyes narrowed, and he moved faster than she could track. In the next coherent moment, she was facing the wall, his chest pressed tight to her back. He brushed his face against her shoulder and inhaled deeply.

She snapped her head back and butted him hard. "Let go of me, you—"

Her breath whooshed out at his answering blow, and she found herself pinned to the wall. Jen shuddered at the blood soaking through her T-shirt.

His blood. The fact that he was bleeding on her sent a shudder of revulsion through her.

"She's telling the truth," one of the others reported. "Maybe we should just kill her with her own weapon and start to search for the pup."

Claws hooked the back of her shirt and tore, leaving light scratches in their wake. Dark laughter from the one pinning her to the wall followed.

"That won't be necessary. We want her alive...for now."

"What? Why would we want a human female alive? Especially one working with the Enforcer?"

"My little brother will give us the Keif willingly if he thinks he'll get her in return." The wolf at her back dragged Jen around to face the others. "It seems Adrien was stupid enough to take a little human mate." He stroked his fingertips over her mating mark and chuckled again. "And she carries his pup."

The feral smiles on their faces made her blood run cold. Jen fought for anything she could say to stop this. "He won't." She wasn't sure if she was trying to convince them or herself. Either way, she couldn't imagine Adrien would ever turn Keif over to them, and she prayed it wasn't so.

"Oh, he will, little one. Any male worth his teeth will do anything he has to if it means safeguarding his mate and young. The Keif is no kin to Adrien. He'll bring us the pup's carcass if we ask for it and walk right into our claws and teeth in a vain effort to save your pathetic hide."

"Like you left Keif for dead and thought it would work? Keif isn't that easy to kill, and neither is Adrien." Common sense told her to stop egging them on, but something deeper and more primal urged her to keep pushing. "You'll regret doing this. Don't doubt it. If you take me out of here... If you lay a single furry paw on me, I guarantee you will pay for it."

One of the others crossed the distance between them in two long strides. The punch to her cheek made Jen's senses spin, and she collapsed into darkness.

****

Adrien parked the car and slid out, weary from the day of tracking. He smiled at the bag he was carrying. If someone had told him the day before meeting Jen that he would be carrying flowers for his mate just weeks later, he would have thought the wolf was mad. Yet, he was, and he was happy about it.

The whiff of wolf musk stopped him short. It wasn't a pup's musk. His heart pounding, he charged for the door and launched through the open—and damaged—door frame.

The scent of gun powder hung heavy in the air, and the butt of the discarded weapon peeked from the hallway. Blood added a copper tang to the atmosphere, and Adrien dropped the flowers on the table and started across the room.

He tried to calm himself. *The one who moves in haste loses the battle.* Visions of Jen's crumpled body weren't helping him stay calm. His certainty that they'd killed his mate and pups had Adrien on the edges of a killing rage, snarling already.

The hallway was empty, though he'd wager she got off several shots at the wolves attacking her. The blood in the hall was wolf blood.

None of Jen's? That made no sense. *Unless they sensed that she is mine and bearing, in which case, they don't dare harm her.*

The rooms were empty, though it was clear the wolves had mounted a comprehensive search of the cabin. The entire place reeked of intelligent mark. They'd come in force. At least four of the curs. Surprisingly, he could identify three separate dens: Morgan's, Draven's...and Tragen's.

But not Tragen himself. Adrien took his time, trying to separate the scents. The blood was from his own den. *Viktor. Damn my older brother. He's wanted Tragen's place for years, but he couldn't win against the old buck. With a Keif, there will be no Tragen, and being a den leader is beneath Viktor's aspirations.*

He looked around the cabin again, confused. Jen wasn't there, and neither was Michael. This didn't add up.

They wanted to kill Michael. They wouldn't have captured both of them and taken Jen along to care for the pup. Ransom was cowardly and wouldn't result in them keeping control of their own dens or the pack, as they hoped. What possible reason could they have for—

"Are you ready to hunt, Enforcer?"

Michael's voice shocked him into motion. The pup had come in behind him, silently, stealthily.

Just as I taught him. "Where is Jen?"

"They took her. I couldn't protect her alone, and they used a machine to block her phone. Are you ready to hunt them?" he repeated.

"Do you know where to find them?" Adrien added prayers to Mother Moon that the Keif had had a vision.

"Your brother left a note for you."

He looked around for it, trying to comprehend how he'd missed it. "Where?"

"I read it and got rid of it."

Fury burned in Adrien's gut. "Why would you do that?"

"Because you will try to leave me behind when you go after them. That is not going to happen, Enforcer. They want me, and they want you to bring me to them to trade for Jen. Bringing me is what is supposed to happen, but you will resist doing it. I know where Jen is, and I know I am there when we get her back. We will get in your car. We will call Draven and Morgan and have them bring their best with them. And we *will* get Jen back and make them all pay."

Part of him wanted to put the pup through the wall for playing games with Jen's safety. The other half wanted Jen back too much for that. "Get in the car," he growled.

He turned and padded away on bare feet. "My things are already in there."

Michael took the front seat and buckled himself in. Adrien headed down the dirt track, fisting the steering wheel tight in his hands.

It took him until the second turn to rein in his anger enough to address the Keif again. "If Jen has a single bruise—"

"You mean more," he interrupted. "She already has a few bruises and several scratches." Michael turned his head, his expression promising death to someone. "I know who did it, and they will both die today...painfully. But no...Jen will not be injured further by them." Before Adrien could ask for their names, Michael continued. "Neither will die by your hand, but you will repay one in kind before he dies."

"You knew this was going to happen," he guessed.

"Yes, and I knew Jen would suffer the least damage this way. Believe me, no other path ended well for her."

Adrien shuddered at the thought of losing her. He turned onto the main road into town. "Where are we going?"

"Your birth den."

Another shudder wracked Adrien. The den had been abandoned for a reason. His dam had insisted the den was cursed. Tragen had ignored her, and she'd died in childbirth gone wrong, trying to bring Adrien's younger sister into the world. Adrien hadn't seen the cursed den since he was a pup of eight.

"You should call for Draven and Morgan," Michael suggested.

"What if they bring wolves involved along unknowing?" Adrien asked.

"They won't. No matter how blind they've been, they have good instincts. The wolves they trust are the ones we want there."

Adrien fished his cell phone out and pulled up Draven's den in the contact list. *Mother Moon, please let the Keif be right.*

"I am," Michael whispered.

****

"Are you mad?" Draven demanded. "Bringing Michael here?"

Adrien ground his teeth.

"Do *you* know what's going to happen next?" Michael challenged.

His gran-sire didn't respond to that.

Michael stripped off his button-down shirt and tossed it into the back seat of the car, revealing how toned he'd become in the last few weeks. He'd lost much of his puppy fat and looked like a miniature adult wolf.

Adrien removed both layers of his own shirts, then his boots and socks, and tossed them inside as well. The pup pulled Adrien's button-down shirt back out and tucked it into the back pocket of his jeans. At Adrien's questioning look, he offered an explanation.

"We will need this."

Adrien bit back a half dozen foul curses.

"What is he talking about?" Draven asked, looking up from his own boot laces.

Adrien shot him a glare. "They have my mate. I will *assume* the Keif means to say my mate will require my shirt."

Draven's eyes went wide, and he hurried through removing his boots. That accomplished, he stood and passed a look over the wolves he'd brought with him. All of them were ready to shift and to fight. "We should go in."

"Not yet," Michael ordered.

Draven started to question him, and Michael waved him off.

"We are waiting for the other half of our forces." He turned his head. "And here they are."

Morgan marched into the alley from the side-street. He and his were already barefoot and bare-chested. The old alpha stopped and panned a sour look over Draven and his wolves.

Before either alpha could comment on it, Michael spoke up. "Stop it before you start. You'll just waste time. Draven, you lost your daughter. Morgan, you lost your grandpup. I lost my sire and dam, and they nearly killed me. The rogues have Adrien's mate in there. *All* of us have a reason to seek justice from them. It's time to take care of that. They cannot be allowed to live another day."

He looked up at his great-gran-sire. "You have only one wolf to kill. Leave any others who engage you to Draven's wolves or yours."

Morgan knelt at Michael's side. "Who is this wolf?"

"Your son, Liam. *He* was the wolf my sire told about his suspicions that I was a Keif. *He* was the one who went to Tragen's elder son and plotted my death. *He* was the one who lied to my sire to gain entrance to our den; my sire trusted him and opened the doors to the assassins. They said they came to test me. Liam *must* die today...and quickly, or he will make another attempt."

Morgan offered a tense nod in agreement.

"How long have you known which wolves we were hunting?" Adrien demanded.

Michael didn't look at him. "Always. One does not forget being beaten to near death." He hesitated. "But this way ends well, Enforcer. It had to be this. For Jen and for me."

"If I went for them directly, Jen would have died?" If that was the case, Adrien could forgive the Keif for hiding information from him.

He looked up at Adrien, his expression tortured. "Or been shattered beyond fixing this time. There are some things even a Keif should not see."

That sent a chill through Adrien's gut. "Understood." He focused on the two den alphas. "We go in first. Lure them into thinking I've delivered Michael according to *their* plans. The rest of you come quietly. Don't stop until they are all dead."

"Agreed," the alphas said, nearly in unison.

****

Jen shifted, coming up short as rope bit into her wrists. She opened her eyes and stared at it, her heart pounding. The rope was looped through an iron ring mounted high on the wall.

They did it. They kidnapped me and are holding me hostage to use me against Adrien and Keif.

Movement over her left shoulder sent her closer to the rock wall. She didn't question that it was one of her kidnappers. Who else would it be?

A rough hand clamped tight around her chin and yanked, forcing her face around to him. It was the one she'd shot. It was no surprise he looked to be nearly healed.

His smile didn't reach his eyes, leaving them a steely silver-gray. Jen tried to escape his grasp, and he moved his hand to the back of her neck, holding her in place.

Jen glared at him, daring him to try something. *Anything. Adrien is going to kill you for this.*

He laughed heartily. "Denning females have such spirit. Even when that female is human."

She ground her teeth in fury.

"Nothing to say?"

141

Jen remained silent. He wanted her to talk to him. She didn't intend to play this game his way. The only way she would answer would be if she was defying him.

That's sure to piss him off.

He released her neck and rose, making his way across the cave. "You will need food soon. Water. To relieve yourself."

"I don't want anything from you." Even if she did, Jen couldn't trust him. Anything she ate or drank might be poisoned, for certain.

"But it's my duty to see to your needs. You are a female of my den." It was a taunt, capped with a mocking bow.

She wasn't sure why he was really offering it, but it wasn't out of any wish to make her more comfortable.

He crossed the cave and squatted next to her, seemingly assessing something she couldn't name. "Do denning humans eat meat?"

She'd been craving it since the morning the need for meat had struck at breakfast. At that meal, she'd devoured the entire steak Adrien had put on her plate. She'd come to awareness of her surroundings, chewing the last of the meat from the bone, her face and hands covered in blood and meat juices. Though she'd been mortified by her lack of decorum, Adrien had seemed pleased.

Since then, she'd eaten at least eight ounces of rare beef, cooked chicken or pork, or sashimi at every meal, more than that at many meals. Jen had even woken in the middle of the night and gone to the kitchen, eating leftovers from dinner as if she was starved. Carrying young wolves made eating meat a necessity.

"Oh. You do."

He reached out to push the hair away from her face, and she kicked for his midsection. He captured her ankle in his hand a split-second before she would have connected with her target. To her surprise, he didn't hurt her. Instead, he lowered her foot, then forced it to the floor when she resisted him. His expression warned that she shouldn't attack him again.

His voice was low, nearly soothing, but his words did nothing to soothe her. "You don't understand. It's better this way. You aren't a wolf; you can't understand.

"Adrien tied himself to you. He planted a half-bred pup in you. Your young will be weak, just like you're weak, but Adrien will adore them, because they will be his pups...and yours. My den will be weakened, because we will have to support the half-breeds, to make up for their lack.

"Even if you die...and the pup with you, Adrien is unlikely to choose another mate, and he will be crippled by the loss. Sometimes a quick end is best...for everyone."

Her arms trembled in what she'd like to claim was fatigue. *It's not. It's fear, and he knows it. He's won this round.* "Then why do you want to feed me?"

His smile was cold and calculating. "Out of duty. Out of respect."

"I don't believe you."

He cocked his head to one side, his features hard.

Her heart thumped out a warning beat. Whatever his intentions were, they weren't good. "What?" she forced the word out and put heat on it, trying desperately to hide her terror at his stillness.

"I didn't know humans *had* instincts."

"Perhaps better than yours," Adrien snapped.

He whirled around to face Tragen's Enforcer.

His brother. Jen stared at Adrien and Keif, side-by-side, wearing only their jeans, a nearly matched set. It was a glorious sight. She'd never seen anything more beautiful.

She sobbed in the realization that they'd walked right into his brother's trap. She would see them both, then lose them both.

No. Adrien isn't that easy to kill! But he was so outnumbered.

"Don't worry, Jen," Keif piped up. "Viktor lies."

That made her cry harder, but she couldn't name if it was in relief or fear for them. Whatever Keif saw to make him so sure, it couldn't be flawless. If it was, they wouldn't be here.

****

Adrien reined in his anger at the sight of Jen: bruised, frightened, and crying. *No one harms my mate.*

"Where are Liam and the others?" he asked, certain there was an ambush involved, and Jen was bait for it.

"Close," Michael replied.

Viktor clapped, a slow, irreverent sound that mocked them. "Very good, young Keif. But you don't see everything. Do you?"

Michael shrugged.

Adrien tried not to take that to heart. He reminded himself that the Keif was an adept young liar when he needed to be, for the sake of planning a battle. "Let us end this."

Viktor moved closer to Jen, making a silent threat. "You have no intention of turning the Keif over to us, Adrien. I knew that when I led you in. The only thing I hadn't anticipated was you actually bringing the whelp with you. I thought, after we had dispatched you and your mate, we would have to track the young one down to kill him. How fortuitous that you tried something much more bold. And stupid."

They glared at each other for a moment. Adrien reminded himself over and over again not to be the wolf who attacked in haste. Jen's life and that of his pup depended on him keeping a level head.

Viktor scowled. He reached out and grabbed the back of Jen's fur. She twisted and brought one shoe-clad foot into his knee. He cursed but didn't go down.

The growl from Michael brought Adrien up short, two steps toward his foe. He shook himself out of his mindless anger. Viktor had nearly succeeded in forcing him to move unwisely.

His brother's eyes widened a bit, then narrowed. "The young Keif has learned a new trick since last we met."

The barking and growling let Adrien know Michael had fully shifted. The translation made him smile.

"More than one, traitor."

From the far reaches of the den, sounds of wolves at war reached them. Viktor looked over his shoulder in shock, and Michael moved.

Adrien didn't waste time. He shifted and vaulted past the pup, using his brother's preoccupation to knock him away from Jen. In a flash, Michael was at her side, chewing through the ropes holding her to the wall.

Viktor shifted. His brother tried to circle Adrien, but he moved sideways, letting Viktor close the distance between them rather than letting him outflank him for a clean attack at Jen.

The ropes snapped, and Jen launched to her feet. Michael shouldered her to the wall, then grasped the edge of her shirt in his teeth, urging her down. She didn't question him. In moments, she'd made a ball of herself behind the pup's body.

Viktor came at him, snapping and snarling. Adrien jumped and came down at the back of his brother's neck, wrenching Viktor around and throwing him to the opposite side of the room.

Blood coursed down Viktor's shoulder, and a sound of amusement came from Michael's direction.

"Repaid in kind."

Adrien saw red at that. Viktor had laid an injury over his mating mark? How dare he do something so vile!

"Easy, Enforcer. He will come to you."

Another wolf burst from the tunnels to the meeting room, ragged and bleeding. An older wolf chased him down, knocked him off his feet, and laid fangs into the younger wolf's shoulder, as he took to his feet and ran again, the elder in pursuit. By the scents, he guessed it was Morgan chasing down his son.

Viktor used the confusion to try and bypass Adrien. He wasn't fooled. Adrien raised his paw and brought his claws down his brother's face, laying open his cheekbone and taking one eye. Even if Michael was wrong and his brother survived this, he would forever be scarred and missing his eye.

The resulting yelp was satisfying, but Viktor laid on speed, trying to make a last attempt for Michael. Or perhaps for Jen, in retribution.

Adrien launched himself after Viktor; he laid his fangs into his brother's hip and pulled him down. Before he could go for Viktor's throat, Michael was there, his teeth sending sprays of Viktor's blood flying.

Viktor tried to roll, to place Michael at a disadvantage. Adrien bit his leg and dragged the opposite direction, keeping him at the pup's mercy. He whined, trying to bring his claws up to injure the pup, and the Keif turned out of his reach, forcing Viktor's head further back on his neck.

Michael reared back. Again. On the third time, Viktor's throat ripped out. His body spasmed, then went still, his remaining eye fixed and glassy.

The pup dropped the mouthful of Viktor's throat to the floor, pitched his head back, and howled. Adrien joined him.

He shifted back to his human form and headed for Jen. She lay on the floor, working at the knots frantically. Adrien reached out for her, and she recoiled.

His hurt at that was short-lived. Her gaze met his, and Jen struggled to her knees and pressed to his chest.

"It's okay," he promised her. "I'm here." Adrien untied the ropes, wincing at the bruises and rope burns on her wrists.

The moment her hands were free, Jen wrapped herself around him. She shivered, and he fingered the gaping hole in the back of her shirt. It displayed her back, from his mating mark nearly to her waist. His fangs itched to rip Viktor apart for this.

"Are you all right?" he asked.

She nodded.

"You're cold."

Jen shook her head. "Just afraid for you and Keif."

That made Adrien smile. "My lovely Lioness fears for us, when she has been so injured. I adore you."

Michael appeared at his shoulder, dressed in his jeans again; he passed Adrien the shirt he'd brought in with him. "You should dress her. The others will be here soon."

Right on cue, Draven entered the room.

Michael didn't hesitate. "Draven, go to Adrien's car. The Enforcer needs the medical kit and the food stored in the back seat to care for his mate."

He didn't hesitate. "Right away," he vowed.

Adrien sighed. Responsible wolves protected all females, especially bearing females, even if they weren't part of the same den. The battles between males were never supposed to spill over to the females and young.

A thought occurred to Adrien. He turned his head to glare at Michael. "If you knew we would need all of these things for Jen, why didn't you bring one of her own shirts for her as well?"

"I did bring a shirt. Yours." He smiled widely, showing his still-sharpened fangs. "Come now, Enforcer. You know you want to show off your mate wearing your clothing."

Adrien's move to curse the interfering pup ended at Jen's laughter. He pressed a kiss to her lips instead. Her stomach rumbled, announcing that she'd lied to Viktor when she said she wanted nothing from him.

That is my mate. She laughs while she is broken and hungry. How did I find myself worthy of such a female?

Chapter Twelve

Morgan dropped Liam's body at Adrien's feet. Adrien took a casual glance at it, then panned his gaze to Morgan's face.

The old buck rolled his bare shoulders, seemingly unfazed by killing his eldest son. "The rest will face my claws and teeth within the day," he vowed.

Before Adrien could answer, the Keif spoke up. "I *believe* that is *my* decision."

"No, pup," Draven corrected his grandpup gently. "A Keif does not lead until—"

"He has taken his first kill." He motioned to Viktor. "True, it usually refers to a hunt and prey, but I have killed and I *will* lead."

Both alphas looked to Adrien.

Morgan found his voice first. "Tragen should be consulted," he suggested carefully.

Adrien nodded. "A sound decision. Morgan, take the guilty into custody."

"I will...assist," Draven offered.

For a moment, Morgan looked like he would balk. He shot a sideward look at Michael, then offered his hand to Draven. "You are most welcome to."

Surprise. Surprise. The enemies showed signs of becoming allies.

****

Tragen marched into the abandoned den's audience cave, and Adrien placed a hand on Michael's shoulder in a sign of his protection. He'd run the pack laws through his mind a dozen times, and every time, he arrived at the decision that Tragen had no choice but to let the young Keif lead.

That doesn't mean he'll accept it quietly. To that end, Adrien had questioned the Keif's knowledge of the laws he would have to invoke. He'd also pledged his protection to the Keif anew.

Despite his wishes, Jen had insisted on being present for this meeting, just in case it turned into a confrontation.

The last thing I need is having two people I'm sworn to protect in a confrontation with my sire. Still, Adrien shot her a smile, then focused on his sire again.

As if the movement were magnified somehow, Tragen dragged his attention from the Keif and settled it squarely on Jen. Michael growled, and Tragen's eyes widened in response to the warning. He scowled down at the young Keif.

"You dare—?"

"Jen is under *my* protection," Michael stated boldly.

"Mine as well," Adrien added.

"What is the meaning of a human female's presence at these proceedings?" Tragen countered.

Before Adrien or Michael could answer, Jen's voice issued her own warning to the soon-to-be-former pack leader. "I've been told no one crosses a denning female, Tragen. Not even *you*."

Tragen gaped at her, as Jen pushed to her feet and sauntered between the opposing groups of males. The oversized shirt Adrien had given her to replace her torn one was open between her lush breasts, and Jen had arranged it to one side, uncovering her left shoulder.

And my still-healing mating mark. Had she been a she-wolf, it would have already healed to the pink lines of scar tissue, but she was human, and that would take well over another week.

With her short, dark fur in disarray and the sensual glide of a bearing female, Adrien couldn't imagine a more potent message being broadcast to the males in attendance. *Fuck with me, and I will fuck you over...hard. And that's before my mate gets to you.*

Jen rounded Michael and arrived at Adrien's side before Tragen managed to compose himself and react. The temptation was too much to ignore. Adrien cupped her head in his hand and brought his mouth down on hers for a brief but fierce kiss. His opposite hand left Michael's shoulder and wrapped around her hip.

When he looked up at his sire, Tragen still appeared at a loss for words.

Point one for our side.

His sire recovered at last. He met the Keif's gaze solidly. "I understand, young buck, that you believe you should lead the pack."

"It is the law," Michael replied simply. "Tragen and Tragen's Enforcer are honor bound to follow the laws of the pack, as every wolf is. Further, you are bound to see to their enforcement, no matter your personal feelings about the matter."

"But the laws never intended—"

"Are we questioning the pack's laws these days, Tragen?" the pup challenged him.

His sire shot a look of exasperation at Adrien, and Adrien tipped his head to Michael in a sign of his support of the young Keif. Unlike humans, wolves followed the letter of the law. They didn't argue the "spirit" or "will" of the law.

"Of course we do not question pack law," Tragen snapped.

"Then I lead."

A pulse of nervous tension worked its way through the room. Draven and Morgan prepared to strike at Tragen if it became necessary. At last, Tragen tipped his head in a show of subservience.

But only as far as required. He's not happy about this.

"Which den?" Tragen pressed him.

Morgan interrupted the proceedings. "Mine. Clearly my leadership is lacking."

"Clearly," the Keif retorted. At Morgan's wince, the pup continued. "You would have killed off a quarter of your den and left an entire generation without sires to guide them."

"They knew—"

"But didn't believe it was true."

Morgan gaped at his great-grandpup.

"I *saw* the horror some of them would have displayed at the realization. Adrien and I know which should be killed. The rest will learn from their mistakes."

The old buck nodded and went to one knee. "Then I concede to you."

"I didn't ask to lead your den. This will be upheaval enough for your wolves. They know you as a strong leader. You need to keep control of your den. For now." The threat had been clearly stated. Michael could choose to take that control from Morgan at any time, if he found the den alpha lacking.

Morgan bowed his head deep in subservience.

Draven joined his former adversary on one knee. "I concede."

"I didn't ask for your den either."

Morgan and Draven shot questioning looks at each other.

Michael continued. "Neither den will take me seriously until I approach adulthood. I will choose a den to lead when I mature and no earlier, unless someone forces me to take action sooner."

Draven continued. "It would be best if you took control of a den soon. It is not workable to have a den alpha and a ruling Keif in the same den for a prolonged period of time. Alliances become confused."

"Agreed. I will not be living permanently in either den until I take control of it." He raised one small hand to still the rising protests. "I will spend considerable time at both dens. I have to know the wolves to lead them."

Tragen broke his silence. "Where *will* you den? Who will watch over you? Leader or not, a pup your age must have elders." He stopped short of asking who would care for and guide the Keif. That would have been impertinent.

Michael smiled, showing his half-descended fangs. "I will leave that up to Jen."

Adrien felt his mouth go dry. Had backing Michael put him in a less than palatable position?

His sire beat him to the question. "Jen? What are you saying?"

"Jen." Michael motioned to Adrien's mate. "Jen cares for me, and I protect her. She is part of my den...wherever my den will be. As Jen is a denning female, the choice of *where* she carries her pups is hers."

All three leaders started speaking at once. Michael let them rant.

"You cannot stay with...with another den," Morgan objected. "You must choose one of your affiliated dens."

"My Enforcer stays with me," Tragen ordered.

Oh shit. Here we go.

"We are your family," Draven complained. "You were whelped in our den."

Michael waved them off, and silence fell abruptly.

He pointed to Morgan. "I den with Jen, wherever she chooses to den."

He moved on to Draven. "I don't know what you have been told, but I don't remember more than vague scents of your den." To Morgan. "Or yours. The damage done to me by the assassins killed whatever bonds I'd actively formed before the attempt on my life and the death of my sire and dam."

Draven paled, and his balance wavered a bit.

"I don't say that to hurt you, but the only den I have memories of is the one I have formed with Jen and her mate." He paused. "I will forge new memories in time, building on the scent memories I retain, but at this time, I am bonded with Jen and Adrien and will remain so, no matter what new bonds form."

There was a moment of uneasy silence.

The Keif glared at Tragen. "And you, Tragen, are no longer a Tragen. When the Keif emerges and takes his place as pack alpha—which you have agreed is lawful—the Tragen is no more and neither is his Enforcer.

"I den with Jen, and Adrien is her mate. I trust she will choose a place she is comfortable with—perhaps even familiar with—to den.

"That means, *former* Tragen, that I choose Adrien to stand as *my* Enforcer. Given the situation, I will hold counsel." He nodded toward Draven and Morgan. "The alphas of my birth den and my sire's den will aid Adrien in guiding me." He looked up at Adrien. "I hope Adrien will agree to be my Enforcer and leader of my Counsel."

Adrien tipped his head in agreement. It was the best of all worlds. As Michael's chosen denmates, Jen would be able to stay by the Keif's side. That would make her happy and at ease. One couldn't hope for more with a denning female.

Michael addressed Tragen again. "I honor your den by choosing my Enforcer from among yours. I trust you will accept this honor gracefully."

His expression said he'd like to prove the Keif wrong. Instead, he tipped his head slightly. "Of course, my Keif."

"Excellent. Now that we've made that abundantly clear, we should retire. Jen requires rest after her ordeal. I will tour the dens in the next few days." Michael focused on Adrien's sire again. "Yours last, Reese."

Adrien winced. He hadn't realized Michael even knew his sire's given name.

"If Jen chooses one of the dens, I trust all will be welcome until she whelps."

Morgan and Draven rushed to agree. Reese was slower but answered in the affirmative. Michael glared in challenge.

"My grandpups and all with them are welcome," he grumbled.

Michael reached out and took one of Jen's hands in his own. "Then we should go."

Adrien didn't question him. He escorted Jen and the young Keif to the car he'd left a block away.

Jen hesitated at the door. "Where are we going? The cabin needs repairs. My place?"

Michael smiled. "You know that's too small. I believe Adrien would enjoy infusing your scent into his apartment."

Adrien nodded, his cock coming up at the thought of it.

The pup ducked into the back seat of the car and pulled at the seatbelt, his bare feet dangling over the floor. "Good. We should go."

Jen started to round the vehicle, then stopped and shot Michael a look of suspicion. "You already know where I'm going to choose to den, don't you? All of that was an act. Wasn't it?"

He clicked the seatbelt on and smiled widely. "Of course."

Adrien chuckled at Michael's masterful handling. "Where will we den?"

Michael straightened in the seat, pressing to the back. "Jen's mind won't be changed by anything she sees when we tour the dens."

Adrien shot her a questioning look. "Where will we be denning?"

Her cheeks darkened. "The cabin. Once it's repaired."

"And once the new addition is added," Michael corrected her. "Jen knows what she wants already, I'm sure. Just be sure to add on *two* new bedrooms. I know you're considering one or two."

Jen gaped at him, then nodded. "I'll draw up the rough plans for it."

Adrien pulled Jen into a kiss, his heart light. They would fill those rooms. He was sure of it.

Section Three

Keif's Mate

Chapter Thirteen

"Stop fussing, Amala," her sire chided her. "The preparations couldn't be more perfect.

She swallowed a growl and rearranged the cushions in the guest chamber. Of course her sire was blind to how important this visit was to their den. They'd welcomed other den alphas, but this wasn't a den alpha. It wasn't even the Tragen or the Keif's representative council. This time, they were hosting the Keif, himself.

Amala moved on to the table, smoothing the linens and checking the food she'd personally prepared for the young leader. Everything would have her personal attention. There was no perfection perfect enough.

Keifs were only born once every few hundred years...sometimes once in a millennium. They were beyond alphas, nearly gods walking amongst the wolves.

Or perhaps messengers from the gods. It was said Keifs had mystical powers, that they saw things before they happened.

In the twelve years since the Keif had been announced widely and had taken his place, he'd yet to tour the whole of the pack lands. Though she didn't understand why that was, she suspected it was because of the upheaval of the early attempt on his life.

There were only whispers of rumors about that, of course. Horrifying stories of traitor wolves with no respect for the power a Keif held. It was said that the Keif and his Enforcer had killed those responsible, but at great loss of life. The aftermath of it had left several dens severely compromised, she'd heard. Perhaps he'd seen it as his duty to stabilize those dens before casting his gaze upon the less problematic portions of his pack.

Amala wondered how old he was. A Keif normally took his place after his first successful hunt. He could be as young as twenty-seven, not much older than her own twenty-three years. But chances were he was older than that. She envisioned a heavily-muscled alpha buck in his early to mid-thirties.

"Rev," one of the adolescent wolves called out. "They have arrived."

"I will be a moment," her sire replied.

The young male loped away, no doubt honored to pass messages for the den alpha and the Keif.

Oh, Mother Moon! They're here. Her heart thundered in her chest.

"Amala?"

"I should meet the Keif's party here. Everything must be perfect."

He sighed. "As you wish, of course."

She heard him withdraw, but Amala didn't turn to watch him go. Instead, she fussed with one thing after another.

The rustle of fabric behind her caught her by surprise, and she spun around. Amala gaped at the sight of a young male stretched out on the cushions, his booted feet shedding dirt on the spotless chamber floor.

She was halfway across the sleeping den before her actions resonated in her anger-soaked brain. She snatched the cushion from behind his head a heartbeat later.

His head thumped back, and his eyes went wide. For a long moment, they stared at each other.

Whoever he was, the male was very young. Too young to lead the entire pack, which meant there was no way this was the Keif. Perhaps he was one of the Enforcer's young ones.

His dark gold fur stood in spikes atop his head, and he wore a faded Green Day T-shirt and blue jeans that looked like they were about to shred.

Decidedly not the Keif. Leaders are more conscious of appearances.

He smiled, and Amala snapped her attention back to his face. Her cheeks heated, and she shifted from foot to foot. Had she really been checking out his jeans? What must he think of her?

Her outrage unglued her tongue. "You should not be here," she informed the interloper.

He looked around at the chamber. "I was told—"

"This chamber is for the Keif. Enforcer and entourage are in the adjoining chambers." Amala motioned that direction with a tip of her head, the cushion held tight to her chest. For some reason she couldn't name, Amala was shivering.

The infuriating male threaded his fingers behind his head and settled deeper into the cushions.

Amala fought to produce words. *The gall of him! How dare he ruin all my preparations this way!*

She swung the cushion for his face, frustrated beyond words. A squawk escaped her lips at the hand closing around her wrist and wrenching her arm back.

Her target's smile disappeared, and he shot to his feet, every muscle tensing to pounce. "Release her, Adrien."

There was a bark of order in his tone that sent warning shivers down her spine. This was no half-grown pup. Worse, he commanded with ease. He commanded someone with even more stealth than he himself possessed.

Adrien? Was that the Keif's Enforcer's name? The huge male had visited several times in preparation for this visit, but Amala wasn't certain of his name.

The cushion was ripped from her fingers, and the hand released her wrist. Amala stood there, trembling, staring at the young male's eyes.

Mother Moon, tell me I haven't just attacked the Keif. Please. I will give anything to be incorrect right now.

He eased a notch and his lips parted, as if he meant to speak.

Her sire's voice emerged first. "Is there a problem, my Keif?"

Oh no! No! No! No! How much damage have I done to my den? Can it be undone? At what price?

"No problem at all, Rev," the Keif lied. "Everything...is perfection."

But it wasn't.

Looking into the Keif's eyes was abruptly painful. Amala turned, bumped past the Enforcer, and ran. It was foolish. Where could she go that the Keif didn't rule? Why would she run when she had to make this right?

But run she did...through the chambers set up for the Enforcer and his family members, down the tunnel, and to her own chambers.

It was only then that she realized tears were coursing down her face. *Why shouldn't they be? How could I have done something so rash?*

Someone stopped in the doorway behind her, but Amala didn't look back at him. It was either the Enforcer, here to warn her never to raise a hand to the Keif again, or her sire, questioning her abrupt departure. She didn't have the heart to look her sire in the eyes after what she'd done. She didn't dare to look at the Enforcer.

"I apologize for Adrien. He went too far."

Amala whipped around, her breathing going choppy at the sight of the Keif. She knew she should tip her head, perhaps go to one knee in a belated sign of subservience. Her body balked at either command. She stood there, silent and motionless, as the Keif strode toward her.

His golden eyes held her spellbound. One slightly-roughened hand cupped Amala's face, and the Keif wiped at the closer track of tears.

His voice emerged as a whisper, warming her lips. "The game went too far. I only meant to tease you. I never meant for Adrien to—"

"I apologize. I didn't know you were the—"

His lips brushed hers, stealing Amala's words. She let her eyes slide shut, and her head eased back on a neck that abruptly felt too weak to perform its duty.

A moment later, his mouth came down on hers, ravenous. Amala parted her lips to meet him, gasping at his taste mixing with her own. His tongue rasped past hers, no doubt savoring her flavor as she savored his.

He withdrew abruptly, leaving her senses reeling. The Keif pressed his forehead to hers, his breathing ragged.

"Not the right time and place," he whispered. "Soon. So soon." The Keif backed away a step, his hands wrapped around her upper arms, as if to steady her.

Her move to question that ended at the sound of her sire's voice. "Amala?"

"Here," she offered lamely.

"Is anything wrong?" he pressed.

Wrong? Her cleft was hot and wet, begging for the Keif's cock, and she wasn't certain when that happened. Her nipples were hard and pressing out against the damned ceremonial dress, and she was sure the Keif knew it all. Amala wasn't certain how she felt about that.

The Keif answered for her. "I came to make sure Amala was well...and to request a tour of your lands after I have a chance to eat."

Amala forced her brain to function. "I can arrange—"

"You."

Her mouth went dry. "Of course, my Keif."

He winced, but his expression smoothed almost before she noted it. "Soon, Amala. Soon." With a tip of his head, he was gone.

Amala stared after him, trying desperately to understand his enigmatic words.

"*Are* you well, Amala?" her sire asked. There was something guarded in his expression.

She forced a smile to her face. "The Keif is very...unusual. He unnerves me." It wasn't a lie. It wasn't the whole truth either.

"You try too hard," he counseled. "Relax."

"I will," she lied.

****

Adrien looked up as Michael entered the chamber Amala had run from.

As he'd expected, Jen and Adrien's twin sons were busy eating the food left for them. At eleven years old, Andrew and James were walking stomachs, trying to pack on their full adult bulk as quickly as possible. The twins' younger sister, Jannie, ducked between them, grabbed a handful

167

of the meat, and ran for their room. She stopped at Michael's side, smiled up at him, and offered a cube of the meat.

He laughed and accepted it. "Run, before your brothers eat all of this food and start searching for more," he counseled.

Jannie didn't hesitate, though it was unlikely the boys would be so bold as to try and steal from a pup. In a moment, she was out of sight, most likely seeking her dam's company.

Though he wasn't hungry, Michael popped the meat in his mouth, groaning at the tang of Amala's flavor renewing his sense of her. *She prepared the meat herself.*

"Good?" Adrien asked.

Andrew answered before Michael could. "Really good."

"Why don't you two go find food elsewhere and stop eating all of the *Keif's* food?"

As if that will work. All three of Jen and Adrien's children had been raised as younger siblings to Michael. No one in the Enforcer's family stood on ceremony with Michael, Keif or not.

James looked up, speaking through a mouth stuffed with meat. "If Michael wants it, he can chase us off himself."

Michael and Adrien shared a smile, and Michael lunged for the two adolescents with a growl. The two scattered, and Adrien chuckled at their hasty retreat.

That settled, Adrien strolled to the table and plucked a cube of the meat up. He popped it in his mouth and raised an eyebrow.

"Our young hostess prepared this herself."

Michael returned to the cushions, reveling in her scent on them. "I know it."

"I wouldn't have harmed her." A second cube disappeared into his mouth.

"You had no right to touch her. It was a cushion, and I was just playing with her."

"She wasn't playing with you."

"After all your training, do you really think I would have let her hurt me?"

Adrien sank into a crouch that said he was ready to pounce. "It isn't wise to let your guard down. There has never been a Keif as young as you are. There are those who would benefit from you not living to see another birthday."

As if I don't know that. His council had hidden the truth of Michael's age from the dens not affiliated with him to avoid another attack on him before adulthood. It had been a shock for them to learn he'd taken power so early in childhood, once they met him.

Like Rev, most of the den alphas were older wolves, and the idea of taking orders from a barely-adult Keif ruffled their fur the wrong way. His first official tour of the dens in his pack had been stressful for everyone involved.

Thankfully, Kole was still a young alpha. He'd taken control of his den at only twenty-five years old, so he understood the pressures and the gain of a young leader.

"Amala isn't one of them." Michael was confident of that.

His Enforcer's gaze narrowed. "Something I should know?"

"She will be taking me on a tour of Rev's lands after my meal." Not that he wanted food.

"I will be ready to—"

"Alone." Michael stressed it, warning his Enforcer off.

"Something I should know?" he repeated.

"Nothing you *need* to know at this time," Michael countered.

Adrien looked as if he wanted to argue, but he held his tongue. He rose to standing, tipped his head, and started to turn away. "Guarding you was easier when you didn't hide things from me."

"When was that, Enforcer?" Michael teased.

He cracked a smile. "Oh, yes. This is my Keif. That has never happened before."

Michael laughed heartily at his Enforcer's retreating back. Then he closed his eyes and drank in Amala's scent. *Soon. Very soon, I will be exploring her body.*

Chapter Fourteen

"This is your hunting ground?" Michael asked, though he surely knew it was.

"One of the best the pack has, I am told," she informed him.

"I don't doubt it. I haven't seen its equal yet."

She forced a smile for him and led the way further into the ceremonial wood. Amala worked her lower lip between her teeth. She owed the Keif an apology, but she hadn't managed to offer it yet.

Do it. Do it now. "About earlier," Amala hedged.

She turned to him, gasping at how close the Keif had moved. *Silently, on his bare feet. Without me knowing it. He would be Hell walking in battle. Especially coupled with his Enforcer.*

"Yes. About that." His lips came down on hers.

Amala reacted without hesitation, accepting him into her mouth when part of her wanted to run again. *I should stop this.*

But there seemed to be no reason she could name to do that. Moreover, her body opined that there was no better way to ease tensions than with a hard fuck.

As if he agreed, the Keif backed her across the meadow to the ancestral tree. Then his head came up, his golden eyes nearly glowing in the semidarkness.

The intensity of his gaze made her heart stutter. *I'm prey.* She'd never been prey in her life.

Amala was daughter of the den alpha. *This is the Keif.* Simply put, he was the first young, unmated buck she'd ever met who outranked her sire.

"You ran from me earlier," he stated.

Amala winced, then nodded. His meaning was impossible to miss. Bucks liked a chase. They lived for it. By running, she'd enflamed his interest. She'd challenged him to catch her.

"I will not permit you to run from me again, Amala." He pushed his hips to hers, his cock hard and announcing his intent. "If you are not receptive to what I am going to do, now is the time to refuse me."

Part of her screamed to do just that. Refuse him. Let him know that being Keif didn't mean he owned her personally.

A more primal part of her urged Amala to allow the Keif to sate himself. He was a buck enflamed. He would lose interest quickly enough when he'd sated his needs.

Worse, I attacked him earlier. His ego is bruised. He needs to feel acceptance after my rejection. Males were notoriously easy to offend.

I wanted to know what I could do to make right the damage I'd done my den. This would do it. Amala nodded her agreement.

He answered in kind, then peeled off his T-shirt and hung it over the lounging branch behind her. His body was lean and hard. Amala had no doubt it afforded him speed and stealth on the hunt.

It took Amala a moment to realize she was rapt on the view she had of his bare chest. She moved her attention to his face, unnerved by his stillness.

The Keif guided her to the side, so his T-shirt was behind her, providing a bit of padding for her back. He kissed her, his fingers playing at the thin straps at her shoulders.

The ceremonial dress was a flimsy confection that made Amala feel like a sacrifice to the gods might have in ancient times.

He pushed the straps away and dragged the smooth, woven fabric down her chest. His mouth left hers, trailing the heat of his breath down her throat.

The first suck at her breast convinced Amala that she had never before and would never again encounter a more pleasurable way to make amends for a transgression.

The Keif wasn't gentle about his touching. He was a buck on the hunt, laying claim to prey he'd chased down. He nipped at her nipple, growling at her gasp.

Amala brought her hand up, tangling her fingers in his fur. She urged him on in half-words and halting phrases.

The Keif dragged up at her skirt, then lifted Amala by the waist to lay her across the lounging branch. The position left the hard nubs of her nipples jutting into the cold, night air and opened her core to him.

He came at her like a starved wolf, licking and nipping at Amala's flesh. She tightened her grip on his fur, drawing the Keif in.

"Please. Please, my Keif."

He withdrew suddenly and loomed over her. Amala stared up at him, shocked by the reversal.

At last, he spoke a single word. "Michael."

She shook her head, confused. What was he asking?

"You will not call me Keif, Amala. My name is Michael, and you will use it."

She started to balk at it. He was Keif of the pack. It was unseemly for her to use his given name.

Sense stilled her tongue. What buck would want a female calling out his title during sex? No male she would want to follow, for certain.

Amala nodded. "Yes, my—"

He glared at her.

She swallowed hard. "Michael." *By the blessed Goddess, do not let me say his name in public after this night.* There would be questions, rumors, and all manner of stories spun about them.

Not that it was anyone's business when two adult wolves indulged in a fuck, but when one of them was the Keif and the other the daughter of a den alpha, stories would run rampant.

He stood there, seemingly waiting for something she couldn't name.

At length, his meaning became clear to her. "Please, Michael."

Without looking away from her face, he reached down and pulled the button fly on his worn jeans open, releasing his cock. Amala had just enough time to focus on it before he was in motion.

****

Amala's gaze shifted to his ready cock, and Michael savored her interest along with her use of his given name.

Though he knew she would comply before he demanded she use his name, hearing her say it sent a little thrill though him. It had taken Michael years to accept Keif as a title and not his name. Now that he had, it seemed everyone but his family wanted to call him Keif.

She is my mate. I will not stand for Amala calling me by my title. Ever again.

Michael sank to a loose crouch, drinking in her musk, tasting her female tang, imprinting his mate's flavor on his senses. Her hand returned to his fur, urging him on.

The challenge was on; he had to make her his own as quickly as possible. After the dreams of the last two years, he knew he wouldn't last much longer without her in his life. In this case, his powers had worked against him. He'd barely met her, and already he was surrendering his freedom as a buck to Amala.

The she-wolf in question cried out her climax, her flavor making his head spin.

I cannot wait. He didn't ask if she was ready for more. She was his, and she'd agreed to that, of a fashion.

Michael came to his feet between her thighs and thrust deep inside her. Her claws came up in a defensive show. He'd expected it, so it was no problem for him to capture her hands and pin them to the tree limb. Better that than have to explain his inattention to Adrien or—worse—have to talk his Enforcer down when he returned with injuries on his person.

Amala made no further move to unseat him. On the contrary, her claws retracted, and she gasped out his name.

Not my damned title, but my name. Thank Mother Moon for that.

He thrust again and again, reveling in her body's welcoming flutters, in her thighs tightening against his. He felt her climax coming an instant before it was a reality, anticipation borne of hundreds of dreams of his mate.

There was no holding off. Once her climax was a reality, his followed in its wake. In moments, they were locked together in the age-old union of wolf to she-wolf.

Michael growled. He needed more. He needed all of Amala.

Now. Now. Now, damn it all!

His cock subsided, and he withdrew. He knew what he wanted now. Though he knew it wasn't the smartest move available to him, there was a slight chance of success.

Michael lifted Amala and turned her, so she stood on tiptoe, her abdomen cushioned on his shirt. He was back inside her before her squeak of surprise was fully formed. It ended on a moan, as he started stroking her toward another release.

His fangs descended, and his rational mind scattered.

****

Amala moaned. Young bucks were a delight. They were tireless in their pursuit of sex, and what female didn't love that?

I certainly do.

Michael put his entire body into the task, his lean muscles flexing and clenching against the length of her body. The heat of his seed soaking into her channel, massaged in by the length of his cock working her hard, said he was a more than passable lover, a male she wouldn't mind sharing herself with again, transgression to repay or not.

"You are mine, Amala."

His whispered words puffed across her throat, raising little shivers of delight. Oh, yes. Michael was a young alpha buck, and she was so happy to have been captured by him when she ran.

The scratch of his sharpened teeth against her shoulder shocked her from the bliss of his masterful sex. He meant to mark her, to claim her. *A wolf I don't even know.* "No." She moved to unseat him.

Michael pressed her forward, over the branch, and thrust deeper. His hands closed around her wrists, and growls of warning stilled any fight she might have made.

After a moment of silence, he forced human speech. "If you are refusing my claim, I will accept that. For now. It was a slim chance that you would allow me to mark you so quickly." He gentled his thrusts, stoking the passion she'd thought had fled at his show of force.

"For now?" she challenged. How dare he demand her agreement this way! She was Amala, daughter of Rev, young alpha female of the den. No male demanded of her.

He tasted her throat, and her heart stuttered. It was an overt show of his power. Michael could rip out her throat in this position, but he was nuzzling and licking instead. She didn't want to be charmed by it, but she was.

"For now." It sounded like a concession. "I know well enough what you are to me. In time, you will know it too. It will be difficult to give you that time, but I will. You are due that much."

Before she could speak, he scratched at her throat, low and near her shoulder, with one fang, just hard enough to draw blood. Michael latched his mouth to the spot and suckled up a few drops.

Amala wanted to protest his presumption. The words stuck in her throat. She groaned her approval, her body heating at the intimacy of him tasting her blood.

She knew what he was doing, of course. She'd refused his claim mark. He was taking a taste of her, proving that she wouldn't fight him when he did.

Proving he has this power over me. It is a matter of ego for him.

Moreover, he was imprinting her taste on his senses. Michael would be able to track her unerringly. For the same reason, wolves often took a taste of their young. It was a sign of protection. And of possession. Some traitor corner of her mind wanted to be his possession.

That was all it took to send her over into climax again. Michael joined her. His cock locked into her body, reminding her that he wanted more from her.

His grip on her wrists loosened, though he didn't withdraw. Was he afraid she would attack him? Or was he simply offering proof that he knew she wouldn't?

"I know you will refuse more tonight, Amala, but I am resolved to ask anyway."

She didn't reply to him. With her mind and body at war over the answer she should give, how could she answer him? What should she say?

He already knows I will refuse him. He's told me what I will say. Perhaps he was indicating that he didn't want her to agree for the wrong reasons or to agree when she wasn't certain what she wanted to say. He would be a strange male to say such a thing, but he wasn't a typical male. He was a Keif, and he'd been raised with a human dam.

His cock subsided at last.

Too soon. I want more time.

As if denying her, Michael eased out of her body and turned her toward him. "Do you want to accept more of me tonight?" he asked formally.

"No." The lie came out shaking and weak, and her heart ached at uttering it.

He tipped his head. In the next moment, his lips were parting hers. Amala gave herself over to the kiss, her body demanding more of him.

Michael released her and took a step backward, his fur laying half-over his golden eyes. "I know that is a lie, but I also know you are unsure. Go. Now." He pointed the way.

Amala stared at him, stunned by his rejection of her.

"If you stay, I will take all you give, though you give lip service to not wanting it. If I do that, you will be my mate formally before morning, and you will never trust me. You must go."

Her breathing went strangled, and the need to run settled in the pit of her stomach.

He met her gaze solidly, his teeth and claws extended in show of his lack of control. "Go." It came out more a growl than a proper word.

She held the dress to her chest and bolted the way they'd come. Amala tripped over her own feet at the sound of a howl behind her. She turned back, half expecting to see Michael running her down. Instead, she saw his wolf, glorious and powerful, running for the trees.

At his second howl, she ran full out, stopping only to clean herself in the river before she made her way back to her rooms. In the darkness, she lay on the mattress, shivering within the cocoon of her blankets.

I am his mate. Amala had never considered finding a mate from another den. She'd thought she would live in this den her entire life. Was being with Michael worth leaving her home and family?

She suspected it was, and that scared her more than the rest combined.

Chapter Fifteen

Michael snapped awake, coated in sweat and shaking hard. He buried his face in his dam's cushion, much as he had when he was a pup. He wished it still held her scent, but some things didn't last.

The important things seldom do.

Visions like this one always left him feeling drained. *It has since the first one. The fatal one, if one could pardon such a weak pun.* He'd had visions of the assassins, visions that had snapped him awake in a similar sweat.

Too late. The assassins had already been inside the doors. It had been far too late to stop what he'd seen coming for them. *The frustrations of being such a young and untrained Keif.*

I have to be sure. Michael followed the visions from one choice he could make to others. It was always like this. The decisions of others were a given. How his own actions and words affected those decisions were the only variable he had to take into account.

"Is there a problem, Michael?" Jen's voice came from the doorway between their rooms, shocking him out of yet another possible future.

He didn't question what had drawn her. Even after all these years, her sleeping schedule was offset that of the wolves slightly. She slept more of the night and was awake more of the day. The fact that she was up and about said the sun was already in the sky.

She checks on me as she does her own young. She always has.

Jen moved closer. "Michael? Are you all right?"

"I need to see Adrien."

She was still for a long moment. Michael looked her direction, meeting her wide-eyed gaze solidly.

At last, she nodded and turned away. "I'll get him right away."

She knows it was a vision. Of course she would. How many visions had Jen seen him wake from over the years?

Thankfully not many like this one.

Adrien entered Michael's sleeping den a moment later, barefoot and bare-chested. He stopped and sniffed the air, his eyes narrowing and his muscles bunching.

"What is coming?" his Enforcer asked.

"I'll need you to perform your duty. This evening, I believe." It might be as late as the following evening, but as the years went on, his sense of the timing of his visions had become honed.

"Should I send Jen and the young away?"

"That won't be necessary. No one will approach them, let alone harm them." None of the possibilities hinted at that.

"Where and when?" Now that Adrien knew his mate and young were safe, Michael was his only concern.

"I will take a walk this evening. I don't know the place...yet." One of the most interesting things about his powers was finding new places this way.

"I'll have to follow you then."

"No. You will follow Amala. She will come to see me."

Adrien swiveled his head, loosening his muscles as if for battle. "I thought you said Amala saw no gain in turning against you." It was a challenge.

"She still doesn't. Others see a gain in using my...preoccupation with my mate to their advantage."

"Your...?" Adrien cleared his throat. "Amala?"

"Now you need to know it," Michael offered calmly.

He tipped his head solemnly. As the Keif's Enforcer, Adrien was charged with protecting not only Michael, but also Michael's mate and young, when Mother Moon blessed him with young from Amala.

"Oh...Enforcer?" Michael put an edge of steel in his tone.

Adrien arched a brow. "Yes?"

"My mate will not need...careful watching. In fact, it might be a healthier choice if you didn't look too closely at her."

"I'm a mated man," he protested.

"As am I."

Adrien fought back what looked suspiciously like a laugh. "As you say, my Keif. As you say."

In the next moment, he was gone.

Off to make whatever preparations he feels are necessary.

****

Amala ambled through the hunting grounds, her mind running in pointless circles. Accepting the Keif as her mate both solved problems and caused them.

Her sire was an old alpha, and she had no brothers. In a situation like that, whatever alpha defeated her sire in battle for leadership would expect to take Amala as mate, were she willing. Since none of her sisters had mated to potential leaders and Amala was the last remaining unmated daughter of Rev, they would see it as a way to pass the leadership without further battle. She knew the contenders, and she was sure to make an enemy of someone, unless a new contender she didn't despise arose in the next decade.

Damn my alpha nature. I could have been safely mated off to an unassuming male long ago, if I had a temperament to match my sisters', but I don't.

If she mated to the Keif, no one else would try to force her to be his mate. Of course, that still left her accompanying the Keif to wherever he ultimately chose to lead, which meant only sporadically seeing her sisters and sire.

It also meant leaving her den in a state of serious unrest. None of the potential leaders would go down without a fight. Without Amala's mating as the deciding factor, there would be one battle for leadership after another...after another...and another. It might mean more than a year of upheaval for the den, before a single strongest alpha emerged and turned away all challengers.

She shivered at the thought of such upheaval. Wolves thrived in the den and pack, not in a den divided.

But not at the cost of mating with someone I don't want.

Did she want Michael?

"Michael." She cursed. Twice already, she'd had to stop herself from saying his damned name aloud.

Not that she'd seen the Keif. He'd kept his distance, since the events of the night before. Her sire said Michael had come in very late, scented of a hard run and a hunt. He'd delivered the kill to his human dam, for her young, and retired to the room Amala had prepared for him.

A noise intruded on her inner thoughts, and she whirled that direction. Amala dropped to a crouch, letting her eyes, claws, and teeth shift for protection. She drew in the scents of the night around her, scanning the tree line in the direction the sound had come from.

Nothing. Nothing moved in the shadows. No scents of wolf or human wafted on the wind. No sounds but the sounds of prey, insects, and birds reached her. She waited a bit more, then stood. Amala cursed herself for being so jumpy and moved along.

The night was chill, and she smiled at the thought of the hot springs over the next rise. Amala took off at a run, enjoying the wind on her face and the grass against her feet.

She skidded to a halt at the side of the largest pool and started stripping off her clothing. The scent of male wolf assaulted her, and she pressed her shirt to her chest.

"You don't need to fear me, Amala." His voice came from the darkness at the far side of the pool.

"Michael." A moment later, she realized she'd lowered the shirt. *Damn it. Do I have to be so inviting?*

He moved closer to her, coming into the moonlight on the close side of the pool. As might be expected, he was nude for soaking. Amala got tantalizing peeks at his body through the ripples caused by his movement.

"You could join me," he offered smoothly.

"You knew I was coming here. Didn't you?"

"Not *here*; one of the fun things about having my particular gifts is following visions to places I see. But, yes, the vision did show that you would come here as well."

Amala considered that. He wasn't stalking her. He wasn't using his gifts to prowl in her wake. He was here before she was. Could Michael be held responsible for the fact that he saw things in advance of them happening? That hardly seemed appropriate.

"Will you join me?"

She wanted to, but she didn't want to appear too easy a catch, either.

"You don't have to accept becoming my mate right now, Amala. You are an adult. I am an adult. There is no law in pack or den that says you and I cannot share our passion, if we choose to."

She peeked up at him, her heart pounding and her mouth watering to do precisely that.

"If you wish to share passion with me," he invited.

"As if you don't already know the answer," she groused.

"I could leave, if that's what you really want." His expression was all mock innocence.

"Which did your vision tell you would happen?" Why she wanted to know was a mystery to her.

He smiled. "That's the funny thing about visions. There's never just one. Minute changes in what I do affects what you do, which changes something else. It's like ripples on the water."

The reminder had her gazing at the water between his legs, but Michael shifted to deny her a good view.

Miffed, she found her voice again. "If you know so much, why didn't last night end the way you wanted it to?"

His smile faltered a bit. "With you in my arms, I didn't stick to what I knew I *should* do. I got greedy. Any chance of having you accept me faster seemed better than waiting for a sure moment in time." He shook his head, appearing weary. "You have no idea how crazy visions of you can drive a wolf. You are a most passionate female, you know, and I know how good things can be between us."

Something in his tone made her heart ache for him, for the foreknowledge he had but no one else did. Amala had no idea what to say. What could possibly ease his burden?

At last, she dropped her shirt to the grass. "I believe I'll join you. I came here for the water, after all."

Michael backed off a bit and gave her room to enter the pool. Amala took her time, removing her jeans with a wiggle she knew he watched in male interest. Then she slipped into the water beside him and settled to the rock bench some industrious wolves had carved out generations ago.

For a few moments, they soaked in comfortable silence. He made no move toward her.

On some level, that irritated her. If he wanted her as his mate, shouldn't he also be pursuing her as such? She glared at him.

Michael smiled. "If you want something, you only need to ask or to take it."

She splashed him, and he laughed. He loved teasing her, and though she would like to claim she didn't like his teasing, it was undeniable that she did enjoy it. Amala could imagine frolicking with him in wolf form, playing in the deep grass, racing...nuzzling each other.

Hearing him laugh lightened her spirit. She could imagine being mate to a wolf who laughed like Michael did.

I like his sex sounds better. He was close enough to touch, and he'd said she could take what she wanted from him.

I do want.

His smile faded, and Michael's eyes dilated. He didn't move toward her, but his reaction said he knew what she would do next.

I don't know what I intend to do next. But she did, somewhere deep inside. Amala moved closer to him. She extended her hand and traced the ridges of muscle down his chest, getting to know his feel.

He gasped, but he didn't try to take advantage of her position. Neither did he suggest what she might do next or tell her what he might like her to.

Having him give her this power over him went to her head. Bucks rarely relinquished power, and she-wolves had to fight for what little they retained in the face of a larger, intent male wolf. She wondered if having a human dam had colored his sensibilities.

No. I have seen the Enforcer's sons in motion. Clearly, having a human dam—or being raised by one—doesn't have that effect on child rearing. It must be because he is a Keif. I've been waiting for a male like this my whole life and never knew what it was I truly wanted.

She did want him, but she wasn't ready to submit to his mark yet. What would the other wolves say if she fell so quickly to a wolf she'd just met?

There is no law that says I cannot share passion with him. She intended to.

Amala stroked her hand lower, circling his ready cock. He growled, and his teeth sharpened, but he held himself firmly in place. One stroke up his length led to a second...a third.

His eyes transformed into wolf form, and a rumble of frustration escaped his chest. She wondered how long she could tease him before he snapped and captured her. Amala suspected it might be some time.

I don't intend to wait that long. Though being captured by him again would be thrilling, Amala wanted to invite him in this time.

"I want you inside me," she admitted.

Michael closed his hands on her hips and turned her toward him on the bench. He pulled her legs wide around his body before she could part them for him. On his knees, he stalked between her thighs.

She sank back to the rock wall, shivering in anticipation. Amala gasped as he lifted her to the head of his cock. There was something appealing about a partially-shifted male showing such control that made her ache to have him between her thighs.

As if he heard that thought, Michael pulled her around his length, his wet fur teasing at her buttocks and core. She whimpered in delight, and her sheath clutched down, trying to hold him as he eased back for another thrust. That one wrenched a cry she would like to deny was submission from her.

What glorious pups Michael would sire!

Amala had never considered life as a dam before, but it hardly seemed possible not to in such intimate contact with Michael.

She labored the heated air in and out, her mind spinning. Michael was more than talented at sex games, and he was everything she wanted in a male. Amala wondered how long she could continue to play with him and not beg him to lay his mark.

Michael stroked in and out of her needing body, whispering to her. Though his words said he was patient enough to wait for her answer, his sexual hunger called him a liar. He would already have his teeth latched onto her shoulder if she'd admitted what she wanted to him.

Still, she wanted to encourage him. Amala let her fangs loose and grasped at his shoulders, bringing her mouth to his chest. She made one shallow slice, much like the one he'd made the night before. Such scratches healed quickly and left no lasting sign. Already, her own was indistinguishable from the flesh around it.

Michael didn't protest her presumption. Neither did he attempt to stop her. One large hand cupped her head, holding her to the cut she'd made, urging her to finish what she'd started. "Do it," his voice rasped out. "Taste me."

His blood on her tongue brought knowledge of the wolf. He was wild and strong, a protective male. *What a mate he would be.* She pulled back, savoring his taste in her mouth.

"Michael, please." She forced herself not to beg for his bite. *Not yet. Mother Moon, let me seem harder to tame than that.*

The wind shifted, bringing scents of her den, the rich scents of blood and musk.

Hunt scents. Male. Warning. Two scents stood out from the group. *John and Louie.* The two males most equipped to fight her sire for leadership.

The fur at the back of her neck bristled. A sexual relationship between her and Michael threatened their plans. Would they want to fight Michael? To kill him? To kill them both? Attacking while they were sexually stimulated was a good way to get the upper hand. *And they came in numbers.*

She opened her mouth to voice a warning, intent on breaking Michael out of his arousal before the attack came. At the first syllable, he moved. Amala caught herself against the wall, confused, empty, Michael's support abruptly gone.

Sounds of fighting drew her gaze around. Michael's red-gold wolf had another by the throat. He bit down and shook his foe, sending sprays of blood far afield. He planted his forepaws on the wounded wolf's chest and reared back, ripping out the other's throat. Michael dropped the dripping flesh and fur with a plop.

Finally, he shifted to his human form and stood over his downed adversary...naked, blood-soaked, and still erect. Amala's heart skipped in excitement at such a masculine show.

"Do you require anything else, my Keif?" The Enforcer's voice came from the darkness on the opposite side of the pool.

She startled and covered her breasts with a gasp.

The Enforcer moved into the moonlight, circling the pool without a single glance her direction. He strolled, dressed only in jeans, dragging two more wolves as if they weighed no more than large raccoons.

"If you can handle all three without me, I believe Amala and I need privacy, Adrien."

"*If* I can? You know full well I can drag these three back and present them to Rev without you."

Michael chuckled darkly. "As you knew I could handle this bastard on my own."

"And that you would wish to," he conceded. Adrien switched both wolves to one hand and grasped the rear paws on the last. "Goodnight, Michael. And to you, Amala Rev."

Michael growled, and his Enforcer retreated with deep laughter trailing behind him.

"I will tell your sire you are safe and well," he shouted back.

"My thanks," she replied.

Michael growled again, showing his teeth to his Enforcer's back. She smiled. It was clear the two were fond of each other. They were playful, despite their relative positions in the pack.

He returned to the pool and sank in beside her. Amala stared at him, rapt on the sight of such a powerful male animal.

My mate. If I let him claim me as such. After battle and sex... No wolf would claim I fell too quickly to a male who protected me this way.

"Amala?" His voice was rough, most likely in continuing excitement.

She came to her knees on the bench and parted her lips to his. Michael didn't hesitate. He captured her mouth in a kiss hot in his need to have her agree to be his.

She groaned at the copper taste of blood in his mouth. He was a hunter, a protector. *He is mine.* Amala broke off the kiss. "Now, Michael. I want you now."

He grasped her around the waist, positioning Amala to take him in again.

"No." It wasn't what she wanted.

One eyebrow went up in seeming surprise, and Michael pulled her halfway down his ready cock. "No? Really?"

She pushed his hands away, then rose on her knees, moaning as he slipped out of her body. She wanted him back inside with as little delay as possible. That a given, Amala turned her back to him and rubbed her ass against him, enticing

Michael to mount her in claim. His cock jerked against her, and a low growl rumbled from him.

"Yes," she gasped out.

He sucked in a deep breath, most likely drawing in her scent. "Are you saying 'yes' to my cock or to me leaving my mark in claim, Amala?"

"As if you don't know my answer," she teased.

Michael leaned around her, then cupped her chin and turned her face toward his. His expression was starkly serious. "I will never make assumptions based on my visions, Amala. I respect you too much for that. I would never forego our traditions, especially not one that means so much to the wolves involved. Moreover, knowing what you will say does not mean I will not greatly enjoy hearing you say it."

Emotion choked her to silence for a long moment. "Both. I want your cock and your teeth. I want to be your mate, Michael. I consider you the most worthy male I have ever met...or ever will meet in my lifetime."

He pressed a kiss to her lips, then released her chin. In the next heartbeat, he was inside her. Amala screamed in pleasure. Michael was always enjoyable inside her, but there was something more pressing about it this time.

He won't stop until I am his mate, and I asked him to do it. No buck relinquished his solitude gently, and Michael was no exception. Amala didn't want him to be gentle. She wanted him to lay claim to her, to mark her as his own, then to offer her his blood in exchange.

Her teeth sharpened and lengthened at the thought of it. Her mouth watered to taste him again.

"Soon," he breathed. "Very soon."

Michael started nuzzling and licking at her throat again, and her nipples came to tight little buds of pleasure, being lapped by the churning hot water. His fangs scraped.

She gasped in shock. "Michael?"

"Shhh... Give me this. I know what you need of me in return. Trust me."

She did. "Yes. Do it."

Only the strongest wolves attempted to mark a female anywhere but on her shoulder. It was a sign of Amala's trust in Michael and of Michael's power over her that she would allow him this.

He is Keif. He is my Keif and my mate. No one will doubt him, while I live to correct them.

Michael bit down on her throat, and she whimpered at the slice of pain. He eased his fangs partway out, keeping his bite open but allowing her blood to flow freely into his mouth; he drank deeply of her. All the while, his cock moved in delicious little arcs inside her.

Climax crashed over her, and Amala closed her eyes to the sparks of color playing at the edges of her vision. Michael reared back, thrusting hard against her contracting muscles, growling deeply.

"Now," he breathed. He lodged himself deep inside her, but he didn't come. Michael turned her at the waist, still impaled on his length. One large hand pulled her face to his throat. "Mark me. Mark me as I did you."

She didn't hesitate. She'd never heard of a male offering his throat to a mate. Usually, they offered their arm...or perhaps the front of the shoulder or chest. No one would see Amala as weak, if she marked him this way. They would be viewed as equals by the pack.

All Michael's muscles tightened down, as she bit, but he didn't move to throw her off. Nearly at the first taste of his wild blood, his cum warmed her. His cock engorged, locking in her body in promise of pups soon to come.

"Drink deeply, Amala. Drink all you want."

She eased her fangs back, letting his blood flow faster. Amala suckled at the coursing blood, energized by it and by how freely Michael offered it. At last, she drew away, watching the flow slow, as his healing kicked in.

He brought his mouth down on hers, mingling the remnants of blood is his mouth with the fresh slick in hers. At last, his cock subsided

"More," she moaned.

"Not here. I intend to carry you to my bed now."

Aftershocks wracked her at the idea of that show. "You don't sleep in a bed," she reminded him. It was an oddity; even among wolves who could sleep in the forest or in caves, most of them slept on a mattress at home.

"I don't. Would it be too uncomfortable for you to sleep in my nest of cushions with me?"

"Why do you sleep in the cushions?"

Michael eased out of her body and turned her. He was silent for a moment, focusing his attention on licking the spilled blood from her chest and shoulder. Just when she thought he intended to ignore her, he started to speak.

"I was in bed when the assassins attacked. I had horrendous visions the one other time I slept in a bed, after that night. I am much more comfortable sleeping in cushions." He shrugged.

Amala leaned toward him and licked at the sluggish trail of blood from the fast-healing mating mark on his throat. "I think I would like to try sleeping on cushions."

"Then we should dress you in my shirt and return to the den."

Her heart skipped. "Will I be wearing anything else besides your shirt?"

"Nothing." Michael didn't explain himself.

Bucks rarely do. Amala wrapped her arms around his shoulders. "On one condition."

One brow went up. "And that is?"

"I get to ride you on the cushions."

His cock went stiff between them. "The first time in the cushions," he agreed.

Chapter Sixteen

Michael smiled down at Amala. His mate had finally given in to sleep, leaving him restless and needing.

As promised, the first time in their shared bed of cushions, he had given her the superior position. He hadn't regretted a moment of it. Her sounds had been sublime, and Michael found he enjoyed giving her the power to take what she wanted from him.

They'd barely recovered from it when he'd rolled her beneath him and taken control of their lovemaking. Between gasps and shouts, Amala had informed him she would have to kill any female he'd been with before her. He'd smiled, though he hadn't admitted what she would find out soon enough. Since he'd started having dreams of her at adolescence, he'd never taken another she-wolf. Instead, he'd had a very active masturbatory life, all to visions of Amala.

For their last time, he did something he'd dreamed of for years. He turned Amala to her hands and knees and pushed her shoulders down to bring her slit up in the way ancient wolves claimed their mates. From the way she made him promise to do it again some night, he guessed she enjoyed it as much as he did.

After that, they'd touched and kissed until she dropped off to sleep, nude in his arms. He wanted more, but he wasn't going to wake her to get it.

Especially since we will have marathons of sex in a week, when she comes fully to her heat. Michael licked his lips at the visions of it, catching his tongue on his teeth in the process.

Knowing he wasn't going to sleep, he rose and padded toward the tunnels. He shifted to wolf form in mid-stride and loped away. If he couldn't make love to his mate, he would hunt for her.

****

Amala curled into the cushions, drinking in Michael's scent on them. By the lack of heat, she knew he wasn't with her, but where he would go at such a Goddess-cursed hour, she couldn't guess.

She listened to the sounds from the adjoining personal dens. She guessed the Enforcer was in his wolf form, playing with his young daughter. His boys were eating, trying to build their adult muscle mass in a hurry. The Enforcer's mate was singing something low and sweet, something she could imagine being sung to a child.

These were the wolves he'd been raised with. Not one of his own dens, but these strangers from other dens, one of them human. Michael hadn't chosen the den he would rule yet, and wherever he chose, she was bound to go with him. While a she-wolf mated to a lesser male might make demands of her mate, the she-wolf mated to a Keif was bound by his duties and position, as she'd been bound by her sire's all these years.

She wondered where she would den, whelp, where they would love together and raise their young. Amala sighed. There was no sense worrying about it. She would learn the answers soon enough.

A clearing throat announced someone's intent to enter. "May we, Amala?" her younger sister Lara asked.

"A moment." She pulled Michael's shirt back on and smoothed it over her thighs, just in case Lara's mate was with her. "You may."

Lara and Jessica, the youngest of her sisters, came in together. Their mates were nowhere to be seen.

Most likely afraid of angering the Keif by approaching his mate in their personal den.

The delightful scent of fresh meat had her stomach grumbling.

Jessica laughed. "I was the same way the morning after mating with Caleb." She set the tray on the floor at Amala's side. "Here. Eat."

She didn't hesitate to do so. She'd reached for a second handful before common courtesy forced her to thank them. "I should have said it sooner, but my thanks for this meal."

Jessica and Lara shot each other looks of confusion.

Amala stopped with the handful of meat halfway to her mouth. "What is it?"

"We only prepared it for you," Jessica imparted.

"I don't understand. Who sent the meat for me, then?" Was it their sire, giving a gift on her mating?

Lara smiled and patted her free hand. "Your mate, of course. He came in shortly before sunrise, carrying a doe over his shoulder, and asked to speak to our sire. Then he asked Rev to have someone prepare this for you."

She took another bite, considering that. Had Michael slept at all? They'd loved far into the night. He couldn't have.

"Where is he now?" she asked. Why wasn't he here with her?

Jessica shrugged. "Most likely still talking to Rev. He is the Keif and has many duties."

"I suppose." Was it infantile to want to be his most pressing duty? She tried to convince herself that it wasn't, but she feared it was.

As if her deep thoughts drew him, Michael trotted into the den in wolf form. He reached up to lay a playful lick on her chin that made Amala smile.

Before she could bid her sisters good day, they were gone. Amala looked back just in time to see Michael shift to human form.

****

Michael popped another slice of venison in Amala's mouth, and she laughed heartily at his play. He'd been worried when he came in to their den together. Something had been bothering

Amala, but whatever it was seemed to have been fleeting.

She curled onto the cushions and placed her head in his lap. It was a comfortable position that made him want to laze about in bed all day.

That sadly wasn't going to happen today. "We have to get up soon. I have an announcement to make before the den, and I asked Rev to hold it in the afternoon, when most of the wolves will be awake and in residence."

Amala wrapped her arm around his waist. "How long will we be here?"

Be here? "Meaning?"

"You have duties, and..." She traced little designs on his lower abdomen. "Where will we den?"

Michael smiled at her tactful handling. She was afraid to leave her birth den, but he'd known that already. How could he not know something so important about his mate?

"Occasionally, we will have to travel to other dens, and I would very much like to introduce you to my family's green place."

She tensed a bit.

"But since I challenged your sire for leadership early this morning...and won, I suppose we will not have to leave this room for as long as we want to. Except, of course, for the announcement of this news to the den."

Amala raised her head and met his gaze head-on. "You what?"

"Rev was quite happy to accept the challenge, I suspect. After all, this will allow him leisure to spend time with his grandpups and to act the role of teaching elder on a more permanent basis."

"You...?"

"I would ask that you accompany me to the green place when you come to heat. I would very much like to conceive our first young there. All our young, should you prove willing."

Words seemed to fail her.

Michael pushed his shirt up her thighs, uncovering her female fur. Her heat enticed him.

Oh, but she is willing.

"There will be peace in the den and in the pack, Amala. I will stand for nothing less, for you and for our pups. You know that."

She nodded.

"Do you know what else I know?" he teased.

She sank to the cushions beneath him, pulling Michael down over her. "Show me."

He laughed. "I knew that would be your answer."

The End

About the Author

Brenna Lyons wears many hats, sometimes all on the same day: former president of EPIC, author of more than 100 published works, owner of Fireborn Publishing, columnist, special needs teacher, wife, mother... and member in good standing of more than 60 writing advocacy groups. In her first ten years published in novel-length, she's won 3 EPIC e-Book Awards (out of 15 finalists) and finaled for 3 PEARLS (including one Honorable Mention, second to NY Times Bestseller Angela Knight), 2 CAPAS, and a Dream Realm Award. She's also taken Spinetingler's Book of the Year for 2007.

Brenna writes in 27 established worlds plus stand-alones, poetry, articles and essays. She's a bestseller in indie/e fantasy and horror, straight genre and cross-genres thereof. Brenna has been termed "one of the most deviant erotic minds in the publishing world... not for the weak." (Rachelle for Fallen Angels Reviews) Milieu-heavy dark work is practically Brenna's calling card, with or without the erotic content.

She teaches classes in everything from POV studies to advanced editing, networking to marketing. Find out more about Brenna at *http://www.youtube.com/watch?v=b61pN_MzszI*

Brenna enjoys hearing from people who read her work and can be reached by e-mail.

Website:
http://www.brennalyons.com/

Facebook:
http://www.facebook.com/brenna.lyons

Email:
brennalyons4168@live.com

Also by Brenna Lyons

Available from **Fireborn Publishing**:

KEIF'S DEN & PACK
Keif's Pack
Keif's Den (Coming Soon)

THE FANTASY CLUB
The Consort (Coming Soon)
Loving the Invisible Man (Coming Soon)
The Midnight Snack (Coming Soon)
A Touch of Mink (Coming Soon)
The Gate-Crasher (Coming Soon)

STANHOPE
Dumb Luck (Coming Soon)
Good Intentions (Coming Soon)

Available from **Mundania Press/Phaze Books**:

We Shall Live Again
Mama's Tales
Marked
Black Sail
Fates War: *Fates Magic*
dan Aidan Fairies: *Fairy Dreams*
Blood Mages: *Enslaved*
Sanctum: *Dream Walk*
May the Best Man Win
Monsters of Myth
The Color of Love
Nevermore

STAR MAGES
Written in the Stars
The Master's Lover

FIRE AND ICE
Magmon's Hunger
Magmon's Lover

BRIDE BALL
Bride Ball
Bride Ball II: Poison, Lies, and No-Win Choices
The Prince's Mistress (Coming Soon)

COUNCIL OF WORLDS: KEGIN
Last Chance for Love
In Her Ladyship's Service
Rites of Mating
Matchmaker's Misery
The Last of Fion's Daughters
Conquest
Earth-Born Lord
Graham: Training the Earth-Born Lord
Double Image (Coming Soon)
Restrained (Coming Soon)
Alien Encounters (Coming Soon)
A Tale of Three Daughters (Coming Soon)
Sivrah Moon (Coming Soon)

COUNCIL OF WORLDS: KIELEN
The Lady's Lowborn Lover
Time Currents
Cubed
Another Man's Lover (Coming Soon)
Cross-Cube (Coming Soon)

NIGHT WARRIORS
Night Warriors
Will of the Stone
Bearing Armen
Hunter's Moon
Veriel's Tales: Crossbearer Turned
Veriel's Tales II: Losing Regana
Starting a War/Choosing a Mate
Raised to be His Own
Blutjagdfrau Lost
Claiming a Lady
Maher Men
Bear's Women (Coming Soon)

ANGEL-WING SAGA
Sons of Heaven: Beldon
Daughters of Man: Prize Match
Sons of Heaven: Unexpected Mates
Daughters of Man: Claiming a Princess
Sons of Heaven: Print Volume 1

UNEXPECTED FATHERS
Unexpected Daddy
Unexpected Granddaddy (Coming Soon)

IT'S ALL GREEK TO ME
All's Fair...
The Only Two Things in Life... (Coming Soon)

CARSON COUSINS
All I Want for Christmas is You
Sabotage (Coming Soon)

XXAN WAR
Daahn Rising
Crossbred Son
Raashh Decisions
Daahn Breaking (Coming Soon)

Available from **Under the Moon**

With Great Power
Undead Underway
Undead Embrace

RENEGADE
Tygers
Renegade's Run
Max Sec
Alpha House (Coming Soon)

URBAN GRIMMS
Catch Me, If You Can
Three Wishes
The Temptation of Eve

Available from **Logical-Lust**

"Mine for the Night" in *The Cougar Book*

Available from **Brenna Lyons**

PROPHECY SERIAL
The Prophet's Mate
Prophecy: Revelations
Prophecy: Rapture
Meeting Gavin
Prophecy: Rampage (Coming Soon)

Beyond the Veil
Snapshot from a Poet's Life
Mine for the Night
The Fire God's Woman
Stay With Me
Overtime Pay

And more...

Award Winning Titles

NOBODY: An Anthology of Dark Fiction
Spinetingler's Book of the Year 2007
Winner

Coming Together: Into the Light [2011]
Coming Together: Against the Odds [2010]
Time Currents [2010]
EPIC eBook Awards
Winner

Bride Ball [2011]
The Master's Lover [2011]
The Cougar Book [2011]
Matchmaker's Misery [2010]
Three Wishes [2010]
"The Fire God's Woman" [2009]
Phaze in Verse [2008]
All I Want for Christmas [2006]
Rites of Mating [2006]
Renegade's Run [2005]
Snapshots of the Poet's Life (WAS Collected Poems,
Book One) [2005]
Fion's Daughter [2004]
EPIC eBook Awards/EPPIE
Finalist

Last Chance for Love [2003]
Dream Realm Awards
Finalist

Night Warriors [2004]
PEARL
Honorable Mention

Will of the Stone (WAS König Cursebreakers) [2004]
Schente Night [2003]
PEARL
Finalist

Written in the Stars [2010]
Joyfully Reviewed, Best Books
Winner

Written in the Stars [2004]
Ultimate Warriors [2004]
CAPA
Finalist

Last Chance for Love [2008]
Love Romances and More Café SF/F Book of the
Year
Runner Up

Prophecy: Revelations [2003]
Treble Heart Award
Finalist

All I Want for Christmas is You
Daughters of Man: Claiming a Princess
Night Owl Reviews
Top Pick